BLINDED BY A WOMAN

All was darkness in the
hear a sound. So far, so g
bent at a crouch turning
someone to burst out of
sound.

He started to the right, free hand sliding along the wall until he accidentally knocked a picture loose. It struck the floor with a loud bang and Longarm froze, certain that someone must surely have been awakened by the sound.

And he was right. He saw a thin bead of light materialize at the bottom of the door. Longarm stepped up to the door and, when it eased open, he flattened against the wall.

What happened next was so sudden that he had no time to think but only to react. A form jumped into the hallway and opened fire with a pistol. Longarm saw its muzzle flash but the one pulling the trigger was shooting blind.

Longarm ducked low and squeezed off a rifle shot. In the closed hallway, it sounded like a cannon and the slug knocked the man backward. Only now the bedroom door swung open and Longarm could see that it wasn't a man . . .

DON'T MISS THESE
ALL-ACTION WESTERN SERIES
FROM THE BERKLEY PUBLISHING GROUP

THE GUNSMITH by J. R. Roberts
Clint Adams was a legend among lawmen, outlaws, and ladies.
They called him . . . the Gunsmith.

LONGARM by Tabor Evans
The popular long-running series about Deputy U.S. Marshal
Long—his life, his loves, his fight for justice.

SLOCUM by Jake Logan
Today's longest-running action Western. John Slocum rides
a deadly trail of hot blood and cold steel.

BUSHWHACKERS by B. J. Lanagan
An action-packed series by the creators of Longarm! The
rousing adventures of the most brutal gang of cutthroats ever
assembled—Quantrill's Raiders.

DIAMONDBACK by Guy Brewer
Dex Yancey is Diamondback, a Southern gentleman turned
con man when his brother cheats him out of the family fortune. Ladies love him. Gamblers hate him. But nobody pulls
one over on Dex . . .

WILDGUN by Jack Hanson
The blazing adventures of mountain man Will Barlow—from
the creators of Longarm!

TEXAS TRACKER by Tom Calhoun
Meet J. T. Law: the most relentless—and dangerous—
manhunter in all Texas. Where sheriffs and posses fail, he's
the best man to bring in the most vicious outlaws—for a
price.

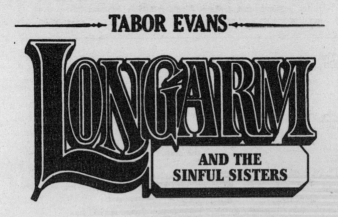

TABOR EVANS

LONGARM

AND THE SINFUL SISTERS

JOVE BOOKS, NEW YORK

LONGARM AND THE SINFUL SISTERS

A Jove Book / published by arrangement with
the author

PRINTING HISTORY
Jove edition / June 2003

Copyright © 2003 by Penguin Group (USA) Inc.

For information address: The Berkley Publishing Group,
a division of Penguin Group (USA) Inc.,
375 Hudson Street, New York, New York 10014.

ISBN: 0-515-13549-6

A JOVE BOOK®
Jove Books are published by The Berkley Publishing Group,
a division of Penguin Group (USA) Inc.,
375 Hudson Street, New York, New York 10014.
JOVE and the "J" design
are trademarks belonging to Penguin Group (USA) Inc.

PRINTED IN THE UNITED STATES OF AMERICA

10 9 8 7 6 5 4 3 2 1

Chapter 1

Deputy United States Marshal Custis Long could feel weariness clear down into the marrow of his bones as he stepped off the train at the Denver depot. He'd just returned from Amarillo, Texas, where he'd had to chase a pair of vicious outlaws before finally trapping them in a desolate box canyon and then killing them after a tough gun battle. He'd been winged in the shoulder and had lost a good deal of blood before getting to a doctor. Now, as he looked for his boss, Marshal Billy Vail, all Longarm could think of was a hot bath, a full meal and about three solid days of sleep.

"Custis!"

Longarm turned with his valise in his hand and peered over the milling crowd of passengers and greeters. Then, he saw her and shook his head in surprise. "Audrey?"

She was tall, like himself, with thick, mahogany-colored hair and dark brown eyes. Miss Audrey Baker worked as Billy Vail's secretary and Longarm had admired her since the day she'd been hired nearly six months earlier. He'd asked Audrey out for dinner at least three times but she was always busy and then he'd learned that she was engaged to be married to a prominent Denver attorney. So, he'd moved on to more available women and hadn't given Audrey much more than an occasional, wistful thought.

"Hello, Custis," she said, hurrying up and looking directly into his eyes. "Billy couldn't make it so he sent me instead."

"I'll have to thank him for that."

"You can do that tomorrow," she said. "Billy is up to his neck in meetings this afternoon, but he'll be free to see you first thing in the morning."

"Fine," Longarm said. "That man has more meetings than anyone I ever heard of."

"They do keep him busy," Audrey agreed. "He tells me all the time that, if it weren't for having a wife and kids, he'd be back out in the field doing what he used to do best . . . tracking down outlaws."

Longarm knew that Billy had once been a top field agent just like himself, but that had been more than six years ago and he'd put on quite a bit of weight since. Maybe Billy could have returned to the chase but Longarm had his doubts. Being a desk-bound official for that many years and pushing a pencil took the edge off a lawman.

"It was nice of you to come down here to the train station and meet me," Longarm told her. "But it certainly wasn't necessary. I could have found my way back to the office and learned about Billy being tied up this afternoon."

"Yes, but that would have been out of your way and when we heard that you'd been wounded down in Texas, the whole office got upset. That's why I'm here to help."

"Even you got worried about me?"

"Of course me," Audrey said. "Why would I be any different?"

"No reason. And I appreciate your concern but the doctor in Amarillo patched up my shoulder."

2

She didn't look convinced. "How long since your dressings have been changed?"

"About three days."

Audrey shook her head. "That's too long."

"I'll be fine."

"I hope so. You know, before I came to work for the federal government, I used to work for a very good doctor. I've changed a lot of dressings and I'd like to take a look at yours right away."

"That's not necessary," Longarm told her. "When I get back to my apartment, I'll take a bath and clean it up. I'll be fine and there's no sense in putting yourself out on my account."

"Billy asked me to take care of you and that's what I'm going to do," Audrey Baker insisted, taking his valise.

"Hey," he protested, "that's kind of heavy!"

"I can handle it."

"Yeah, I can see that, but it makes me feel foolish to let a woman carry my baggage. Audrey, I'm not going to faint from the loss of blood or anything. I'm still capable."

She gave him a patronizing smile. "I'm glad to hear that, Marshal Long. But, and I hope you don't take this wrong, you look very tired and worn out. A little pale, too."

Longarm frowned with sudden concern. "I do?"

"Yes. Definitely. And I can tell you've lost weight."

"Maybe I missed a meal or two chasing those outlaws," he admitted. "But I'm still fit."

Audrey clucked her tongue and shook her head. "Why are you big, tough men so difficult? Why can't you just admit that even you have your own physical limits?"

Longarm pulled his valise back from her grip and said, "I don't like to think in terms of 'limits.' So while I very much appreciate your coming down here to tell me I look like hell . . . I think that it's time I headed for my place and you headed back to the office."

3

If Audrey was offended, it didn't register on her lovely face and she said, "Billy told me to take the afternoon off and make sure that you were all right."

Longarm mustered a tired grin. "If he's given you the day off, why don't you go visit your fiancé? I'm sure that he'd enjoy seeing you every bit as much as I have."

"I can't go see him."

Longarm had been about to walk away when her words caught him by surprise and turned him around. "Why not?"

"Mr. Douglas Johnson and I came to an agreement about two weeks ago."

"And?"

"We agreed that we should end our engagement because we were completely incompatible."

Longarm didn't get it. "You were what?"

"Incompatible. That means that we didn't like *any* of the same things. He was . . . well, I'll not speak badly of him . . . but Douglas was prissy."

Longarm frowned. "You mean he was kind of . . . girlish?"

"Exactly," Audrey said with firm conviction. "Douglas Johnson was a very fastidious man. Fussy about how he dressed and what he required of his meals."

"I only met the man once," Longarm said. "Douglas seemed like a fine fella. He was nearly as tall as myself and I didn't think he looked one bit prissy."

"Oh, he was very handsome . . . like yourself," Audrey quickly agreed. "But he'd been raised as an only child and still clung to the memory of his dear, departed mother, Agatha. And after being engaged to the man for three months, I finally figured out that he didn't really want a mate . . . a woman that would be his wife and companion . . . what Douglas really desired was a replacement for Agatha. I couldn't be that replacement and when I told him so, he got mad and that's when we parted company."

4

"He was quite well-to-do, wasn't he?"

"Yes," Audrey said, "Douglas was very wealthy. He'd gotten his law degree from Yale and his father had been a prominent New York attorney. A very successful one, I might add. I think Douglas might return to New York where he was raised and join his father's law practice."

"So you've given up a lot."

Audrey brushed back a damp tendril of auburn hair that had fallen across her eyes. It was August and warm. "I guess you and many others would think that I gave up the world when I told Douglas good-bye. But I fell out of love with the man and his little idiosyncrasies. He was very critical and demanding and I just had had enough of him."

"Sorry to hear it."

"Don't be sorry," Audrey said. "Because I'm not. Although, I suppose if I were a real schemer, I would have married Douglas and, after a few years, managed to get a divorce and pry loose part of his money. But that's not my style, Custis. Never was and never will be. Now, can we just get you home so that I can look at that shoulder wound?"

"All right, but you're not carrying my valise."

"Suit yourself." Audrey slipped her arm through his arm and they started walking down the street. "You're living in an apartment over on Grant Street just off Colfax, aren't you?"

"How'd you know that?" Longarm asked with surprise.

"As office manager, it's my job to know all sorts of things." She smiled a little secretly and added, "For example, I know that there are at least three women in our office that have an intimate knowledge not only of where you live, but *how* you live."

Despite his weariness, Longarm muttered, "Oh, hell, Audrey. There are quite a few more women than that."

"Oh, I believe you! You see, Custis, being in that big

5

federal office building every day, you get to hear all the juicy gossip. And believe me, you learn *everything* about everyone."

He kept walking, not sure where this conversation was headed and trying hard not to show that his shoulder wound was really throbbing and starting to give him fits.

"For example," Audrey continued, "I know a great deal about you. Not only from what Billy has told me . . . but also from others in the office. Mostly, I might add, women."

"A man should never get involved at his office," Longarm muttered. "I've learned that the hard way."

"You're right," Audrey said, "but it happens. How can it *not* happen? Men and women working together all those hours. Why, it's a wonder the whole building isn't one big love nest."

"Yeah, I guess it is at that. Never thought much about it and I never worked with any of the women in the federal building."

"Oh, but you have! You're required to do a certain amount of paperwork just like the other deputy marshals that go out in the field on investigations." She paused for a moment, then blurted, "And, Custis, I'm afraid that your paperwork leaves a lot to be desired."

Longarm knew that already. Billy was always complaining about his reports . . . to no avail. "I have always hated paperwork."

"That's well-known in the office, Custis. Believe me, I've gone over many of your reports trying to clean them up before they went to Billy . . . or even higher."

This information came as a surprise. "You have?"

"Of course! Your spelling isn't too good and your grammar is terrible. But even worse is the blunt way you state what happened during your investigations. You can't just say that you shot the shit out of someone, you have to say that you were forced to exterminate them in a gun-fight."

"We exterminate rats. We shoot the shit out of killers and other outlaws," Longarm insisted. "And anyway, I just write down what happened without a lot of frills or big words. And if the day ever comes that my reports aren't up to snuff, they can fire me and find a replacement."

"Take it easy," she said, squeezing his arm. "No one is going to fire you. You're the best federal officer in Denver and everyone from the director down to the janitor knows that. Why, within the federal building, you're quite a legend."

The praise embarrassed him and caused Longarm to shake his head and grunt. "Oh bullshit!"

"It's true," Audrey insisted. "All the lawmen envy and respect you and the women . . . well, you *do* have quite a reputation."

They were on Colfax Avenue and there were a lot of people on the sidewalk, many of whom Longarm thought he recognized as fellow employees. Some, however, worked at the nearby United States Mint.

"Well," Longarm said after they had walked three blocks, "here's Grant. My place is right up the street."

"I know."

"Maybe," Longarm said, not sure of what was really going on between them, "you ought to just go on about your business and let me go on about my business."

She looked hurt. "You don't want my help?"

"It's not that," he said, deciding to be frank. "It's just that I'm tired, dirty and hungry. I need a bath, a good meal and a lot of sleep."

"I understand. Just let me take care of your wound and see that it's clean and not infected. If you want, I can cook you up something good to eat."

"I figured I'd go out to eat."

"Not a good idea," Audrey decided. "You're exhausted. Wouldn't you rather I cook something healthy for you?"

"I haven't much food at my place and it's a mess . . . like I am."

"Then I'll do cleaning."

Longarm stopped and turned to face the attractive woman. "Look," he said, "I really appreciate your wanting to help me out but . . ."

Before he could say more, Audrey stifled his protest with a finger over his lips. "Billy is not only your boss . . . but your friend. He's worried about you and he asked me . . . as a favor . . . to meet you at the train station and help you get settled again. He said I was to do whatever was needed to make sure that you were all right. So just let me do that. Okay?"

Longarm was too exhausted to argue. "Okay. But I am a mess and so is my apartment."

"I've seen messes before."

"I'll bet you didn't see any when you were engaged to Douglas."

"No," she confessed. "I didn't. But then, I didn't want to feel like his mother anymore and I was sick and tired of being ordered around all the time trying to meet his petty little demands. So let's forget Douglas and just take care of you."

"Fair enough," Longarm said, continuing on with Audrey matching him stride for stride all the way up Grant Street.

His apartment was in even worse shape than he'd remembered. There were still dirty dishes in the sink that Longarm hadn't quite gotten around to washing before he'd rushed off to catch a train to Texas. The dishes, pots, pans and even a half cup of month-old coffee were covered with a weblike fuzz. The place smelled foul and there were unread newspapers, a bottle of whiskey and an ashtray of stale old cigar butts. His clothes were still rumpled up on the bed and the trash had long since gone to seed.

"I told you it was a hog's pen," he said, noting Audrey's shocked expression. "Maybe you're having second thoughts about staying to help."

She took a deep breath, nose slightly wrinkled from the stench, and said, "Nope. This place just needs some fresh air and a little elbow grease."

And with that, she hurried over to the apartment's two windows, which opened on the alley. Unlocking and pushing them open, she breathed in deeply, then turned and said, "First things first."

"My shoulder?"

"No, a bath. I'll draw the water for that and the dishes, although I think they ought to just be thrown out in the garbage."

Longarm was appalled. "Then what would I eat upon?"

"New dishes," she said, walking over to the kitchen counter and staring down at the crusted and fuzzy organisms that were flourishing on the remains of his last meal. "I'll get you new dishes."

"I don't need 'em."

"Fine!" she said, irritation and impatience starting to creep into her voice. "I'll boil these dishes, pots, pans and the rest and we'll scald away the crud!"

Longarm went into his bedroom and closed the door. He could hear running water in the pipes as Audrey got busy out in his small, untidy kitchen and living room combination. Longarm carefully removed his coat, then grunted with pain as he bent to take off his boots. His shoulder wound throbbed and he was secretly worried that it really might be infected. When he removed his vest and shirt there was a knock on his door.

"Yeah?"

"Your bath will be ready in just a few minutes. But

first, I'd like to remove that dressing and look at the damage."

Longarm opened the door. "All right," he said, going over to his old sofa and collapsing. "But I'm sure it's fine."

Audrey removed the old bandage. There was a sharp intake of breath. "Oh, my," she whispered, "this does *not* look good."

The bullet he'd taken down in the Texas panhandle country had entered his back, so Longarm could not really see the wound. All he knew was what the doctor in Amarillo had told him, which was that the bullet had passed out under his left arm, so the wound ought to heal in a few weeks.

"Does it look bad?"

"I'm afraid so."

"Damn," Longarm said. "How bad?"

"It's serious enough that I'm going to take you to a doctor first thing tomorrow morning."

"It's already been attended to by a doctor. I'm not paying for another one."

"You are even more stubborn than I've heard you to be." Audrey sighed. "I'm going to go find a pharmacy and get some medicines for this in addition to new bandaging. You get in the tub and soak. I'll also get some groceries to cook. Be back in less than an hour."

Longarm started to tell her again that he was going to be all right but, in truth, he didn't feel too well. And this news that his wound was infected just reinforced the idea that he did need her help.

"Thanks," he said. "It's nice of you to go to this trouble."

She leaned over and kissed him lightly on the lips. "No trouble. Not really. It's a relief to help a man instead of a fussy dandy like Douglas. And while the wound doesn't look good now, I think it's going to be fine in a few days.

10

It's fortunate that the bullet passed on out."

"Yeah," Longarm said. "I thought so, too."

"I'll be right back."

As she was leaving, Longarm called out, "There's money in my coat in the bedroom."

"This is on the department," Audrey called. "And so is the dinner."

Longarm didn't know about that. The government was stingy when it came to reimbursements, but he'd let Audrey fill out the damned paperwork.

When the door closed, Longarm went to his kitchen cupboard for a glass, then he poured himself a couple fingers of whiskey. It was good whiskey, too, and it instantly gave him a lift. Then, he found a cigar and lit it before he stripped down naked and climbed in the bathtub. Audrey had found him a clean towel and washrag and, somewhere, a bar of soap.

Longarm allowed the hot water to soak into his weary and battered body while he smoked, reflected on the hard trail he'd traveled down in Texas and the men he'd just been forced to gun down. Killing that pair hadn't been easy and the job had given him no joy. But, in truth, they'd both needed killing and he was glad that he'd not had to bring them all the way back to Colorado where they'd first committed their murders.

The hot water made his eyelids heavy and Longarm turned his thoughts to things more pleasant than killing outlaws. He was so glad to be back in Denver. And once he regained his vigor, there were several women waiting to be called upon. Good-looking women who loved to make love. And he'd insist to Billy Vail that he be allowed to remain in town at least for a month. By that time, he'd want to be on the trail again. Staying in the city too long got on his nerves, although he sure enjoyed meeting the inexhaustible supply of women that Denver had never failed to offer.

Women as pretty as Miss Audrey Baker. Correction. Almost as pretty.

Hmmm, Longarm mused, blowing a smoke ring at his ceiling and taking another sip of whiskey, *I wonder if Miss Baker wants to do anything more than clean me up, bandage my shoulder and fix me a good hot meal? One thing for certain, I won't let her handle me like a mother. Not given the womanly way she moves and looks.*

Thinking about Audrey caused his manhood to poke above the steamy water's surface.

"Down boy," he said with a chuckle. "You're not quite ready for that yet."

But his rod waved in the water and reminded Longarm that it still had a powerful will all its own.

Chapter 2

Longarm was feeling much better by the time that Audrey returned to his apartment.

"Still soaking in the tub, huh?" she called out to him as she placed groceries on his small kitchen counter.

"Seems like the best thing to do," he replied with a lazy grin. "What's for dinner?"

"I'm going to fry us a chicken and I've got corn and carrots along with several other delights."

Longarm liked chicken well enough, though he would have preferred beef. "Sounds good."

She came in to look down at him in the tub. "How's the water?" she asked, slipping her hand in to test its temperature.

"Getting a little cool."

"I'll heat some more. Anything else you need right now before I start cooking?"

"Well," he said, "I could use a little back scrub. With my bad shoulder, I can't reach around and scrape away the dirt and sweat."

"All right. But where is the washcloth?"

"It's probably in this soapy water someplace," he answered, wondering if she would dare to dip her hand down deep and start probing.

"While you look for it and that soap, I'll boil some water and be back in a few minutes. How are you doing on the whiskey?"

"I'm doing fine," Longarm answered. "Haven't felt this good for quite some time now."

"I can believe that. Be right back."

Longarm watched her hurry out into the kitchen. He sure did admire the way Audrey moved. Some women just had the right wiggle to their walk, while others moved like draft horses. Audrey was as graceful and perky as a thoroughbred filly.

He finished his cigar and extinguished it in the bathwater, careful that she wasn't watching. Then, he drained his glass and closed his eyes on hearing her return. When Audrey poured boiling water into the tub, he drew in a sharp breath and exclaimed, "Damn, that's hot! Watch out now because you nearly scalded my most prized possession."

"And what would that be?" she asked, kneeling beside the tub with an expression more of amusement than concern.

"I think you know the answer."

"You mean . . . this?" the woman asked sweetly as she reached into the heated water and found his large and semistiff rod.

Longarm chuckled. "Smart woman. So what are you going to do now?"

She gave his manhood a strong squeeze. "I'm going to scrub your back and clean that wound."

"I can think of things I'd rather you do."

"Custis, I'll just bet you can. But we must both remember that you're wounded."

"What you just grabbed ahold of is feeling just fine,"

he said, getting plenty aroused. "Look, it's even waving at you."

She saw the tip of his pole sticking up just above the water. It was pink from the heat and even though mostly submerged, it still looked big and impressive.

Audrey touched her fingertip to her lips, then placed it on the tip of his rod saying, "You're right. He looks hot, but not hurt. I might just have to take a closer look at him after I finish washing your wound and your backside."

"I'd like that fine," he said, handing her the soap and washrag he'd just found.

She was gentle when she washed not only his back, but also his hair. And when she cleaned around the bullet holes, she was both experienced and tender.

"Custis, I don't like the looks of this."

"What's wrong?" he asked.

"The wound is going to leave a nasty scar and will take quite a while to heal."

"I've got lots of scars, so what does another matter?"

"You're right. I've been studying your back and it looks like you have been whipped with barbed wire."

Longarm knew what she was speaking of. "There was a powerful but ruthless cattle rancher up in Wyoming who tied me up in barbed wire and dragged me about a mile behind his horse. That one was pretty bad, all right."

"He dragged you wrapped in barbed wire?"

Even though he couldn't see her face, Longarm could tell that Audrey was appalled. "Yeah."

"How did you manage to survive?"

"I broke free of the wire and then rolled off the road into a deep ditch. The rancher thought I was finished, but when he rode down to make sure, I gave him the last surprise of his life."

"You just shot him out of the saddle?"

"Sure did. I carry a hideout derringer and I drilled him through his black heart. Then I got that wire off myself

15

and wrapped it around the rancher and dragged him all the way back to town. You see, he had a lot of friends and I wanted to make them understand that I meant business. That a Deputy United States Marshal isn't someone to be taken lightly."

"I'm sure that you left a lasting impression. What about this long scar just to the right of your spine?"

He felt her trace her finger down his backbone. "I believe that one was the result of a Mexican saber. It looks worse than it felt and really wasn't very deep."

"You were sliced by a sword?"

"I never saw the Mexican officer until after he delivered the blow. If he'd been a little braver, I'd be dead, but he fell back after taking his swipe. That was his big mistake."

"And I'm sure it was a fatal mistake," Audrey said.

"Of course. I was in Mexico and had no authority to arrest the man, so there was nothing else I could do but make sure he never tried to ambush a lawman again."

"It's amazing to me that you are still alive, much less able to perform your duties."

"I can perform quite well when I set my mind to it," Longarm said with a wink. "Now that the water is hot again, why don't you undress and climb in here and share my bath?"

She pretended shock. "You can't be serious!"

"I sure am. My big friend that's waving at you shows me that he's serious, too."

Audrey studied the throbbing tip of Longarm's manhood again and then she gave it a little tweak. "All right. Why not? I've never bathed with a man before. It might be fun."

"It'll be more than fun," he promised, feeling his temperature rising.

"I just need to turn down the stove so our chicken doesn't burn. Will this take long?"

"Probably not."

She kissed him on the lips and was gone only a minute or two. When she returned, Audrey was already half undressed. Longarm watched with interest and what he saw was a delight. Audrey had a fine body with long, tapered legs, full breasts and a tiny waist.

"Do you think we can both fit in there?" she asked, eyeing the tub with unconcealed skepticism.

"We can. Trust me."

"So this is not the first time you've had a woman in your tub?"

"That's right and I doubt it will be the last."

She pouted. "Well, I should resist. You have a notorious reputation for loving then leaving women."

"Audrey," he said, "I'd like you to join me in here but it's your choice. I have never paid for a woman and I've never forced one to do something that was against her nature. So make your choice."

She frowned. "That's the Custis Long that I've heard so much about. No nonsense. No sweet, beguiling talk. Just the facts, ma'am. Take it or leave it."

He opened his arms wide. "Are you finally finished talking?"

She removed the last of her undergarments and stepped into the tub, one foot on each side of his hip. "This is going to be a wee bit tricky, isn't it?"

"Not near as much as you might expect. Just take the little red man down there and put him where he feels happiest."

Audrey giggled, then took Longarm's rod in her hand. She gently sat down in the water and it rose almost to the top. When Longarm pushed up inside her honey pot, Audrey sighed and wiggled her bottom until Longarm was completely sheathed.

"Ooh," she moaned, "this is nice."

17

"It'll get even nicer when you start to move up and down."

"If I do that, we're going to make waves and get water all over the floor."

"I got a mop you can use when you're done and I got a feeling that you'll think it was worth the effort."

Audrey closed her eyes and began to move up and down on Longarm's red and glistening shaft. He slipped his hands around to grip her buttocks and closed his own eyes, just focusing on the feeling. As their action grew more vigorous, waves began to crash over the lip of the tub and onto the floor, but neither of them cared.

"Oh, Custis," she whispered, "you're so much bigger than Douglas and as hard as steel. I feel like I've been impaled on the sword of a Roman gladiator."

"Not quite," he said, fingers starting to dig into her buttocks as she moved faster and his pleasure intensified.

Audrey slowed, then quickened again and again, each time bringing them both almost to the pinnacle of their passion. Finally, Longarm began to do his own thrusting and pulled the woman forward to tongue her hard nipples.

"Oh, darling," she cried, throwing her head back and staring at the ceiling with glazed eyes. "Do it! Do it hard right . . . now!"

The power of her climax was impressive and Longarm drove himself deep into her straining body, lifting Audrey almost completely out of the water as he planted his hot, spewing seed. Huge waves crashed over the lip of the tub and ran across the floor all the way into the kitchen.

After a wonderful dinner, they sat close together on Longarm's old couch and nibbled on apple tarts until long after the sun went down. Audrey looked into his eyes and said, "You must be exhausted. I didn't think you were up to doing it twice."

"If you think I was good today, wait until you see me in action tomorrow."

"Oh, good heavens!" she exclaimed in mock terror. "If you do me that hard and long tomorrow, I'll be as bow-legged as an old-time cowpuncher."

"You're a strong woman. You can take whatever I can dish out."

"You think so, huh?"

"I'm sure of it."

Audrey shivered. "When you talk like that, one part of me wants to say, 'Sure I can. Let's screw ourselves half to death. Make love so hard and often that we feel dizzy and wildly wicked.' But the other part of me says, 'Be careful, Audrey. This is a man with a serious bullet wound. And besides that, he makes love so powerfully that he just might split you like a soft aspen log.' "

"You'll survive and want it even more."

"How can you be so confident?"

"I just am," he replied as if that was all there was to say.

Audrey finished off her third apple tart and licked her lips seductively. "Douglas was so . . . so constricted in his lovemaking. He didn't like the messiness of it. The juices, if I can be so plain speaking."

"Probably didn't like his sheets to have spots on 'em either."

"That's right! He always insisted that we put a thick towel down on the sheets before we made love. And afterward, he would fold the towel up and throw it away as if it were something very dirty."

"He sounds like he needed to be educated about making love. Did he ever make you . . . well, yell and go crazy?"

"You mean like you make me do?"

"Yeah."

"Not once. Oh, it always felt good. And sometimes it took a long time. But when he came inside of me he would clench his jaw and make this funny little sound in his throat like he was about to choke or strangle on a chicken bone."

"Maybe he was thinking about his mother. Maybe she was the one that had messed up his mind when it came to a man and woman together in bed."

"I hadn't thought of that, but you could be right."

"Let's not talk about Douglas anymore," Longarm said. "Let's get some sleep. Tomorrow is going to be a fine day."

"You'd have to beat me with a stick to make me leave you tomorrow morning."

"Good. We'll take a stroll around the town and see the shops. Come back here and take a long nap and make love when we awaken. Then tomorrow evening, we'll go out to eat someplace special."

"I can hardly wait," she told him.

"It'll be fun," he promised as he got up, took her hand and led her back into his bedroom.

Chapter 3

It had been their stated intention to sleep late that first morning together. But promptly at eight o'clock, Longarm and Audrey were awakened by a loud knock on the door.

"Who could that be?" Audrey asked, rubbing sleep from her eyes.

"Beats me," Longarm replied. "But if we ignore it, I'm sure it will go away."

"Good idea."

But whoever was at the front door was very persistent. Finally, when Longarm could stand it no longer, he shouted, "Go away!"

"It's me! Billy!"

"Oh, damn," Longarm swore. "It's our boss."

Audrey groaned. "Just what I need. There goes my job, my reputation, my paycheck."

"Climb under the bed," Longarm ordered. "He'll never even know that you're here."

The woman hopped out of the bed and, without bothering to grab a stitch of clothing, fell to the floor and then wriggled under the bed. "It's tight in here and . . . oh no! What is *this*?"

"Hush up," Longarm said as he struggled into his pants.

21

But Audrey wasn't finished. "Custis, it's . . . it's a woman's . . . oh how disgusting!"

"Audrey, be quiet! I'm going to go let Billy in now."

As Longarm hurried toward the door he could hear the woman grousing and swearing. He wasn't sure what she had discovered under his bed, but it obviously wasn't a bouquet of fresh red roses.

"Hello, Billy," he said, swinging the door open.

Marshal Vail hurried inside, not even bothering to reply. He went over to the couch and flopped down looking as if he'd just run a mile up a mountain. His face was red and his chest was heaving. He gasped, "Good to see you, Custis."

"Same here. Sorry I don't have any coffee ready. Maybe we could go out to breakfast later . . . if we need to talk."

"We must talk all right. But I'm afraid what I have to say can't wait."

Billy had a tendency to get excited and to exaggerate difficulties, but this time Longarm sensed that there was a real emergency at hand. "What's wrong?"

"What *isn't* wrong!"

Longarm was shirtless and barefooted as he went over and laid his hand upon the older man's shoulder. "Take it easy. You know what the doctor said about getting over-excited and how it could stop your heart. So take a couple of deep breaths and try hard to relax. Whatever it is that went wrong, it can be fixed."

"I'm not so sure."

"What is the problem this time?"

Billy dragged a clean, white handkerchief from his coat pocket and mopped his sweaty brow. He then blew his nose, folded the handkerchief and placed it back in his pocket. "Custis," he began, "do you remember that trouble we had about two years ago down on the border near the little town of Spur, Arizona?"

Longarm frowned. "I'm afraid I've forgotten. Refresh my memory."

"Well, there was this really powerful ranching family. They own half a million acres or some outlandish amount of land down along the border with Mexico."

"Oh, yeah. The man's name was Brendon Killion and he has this huge ranch named the Black Scorpion."

"That's right," Billy said. "Brendon Killion was a wild, black Irishman. A revolutionary as crazy for power as he was rich."

"Wasn't he involved in some scheme to win back part of southern Arizona for Mexico?"

"That's the one. His wife, Veronica, is related to some of northern Mexico's most notorious revolutionaries, not to mention the Apache that work both sides against each other. I've heard she is still quite a looker but as cold as ice and as cunning as a wolf. They say that she was the real power on the Black Scorpion Ranch."

"What has all this to do with you being here right now?"

"I'm afraid that all hell has broken loose down there while you were down in Texas."

"What does that mean?"

"It means that three Arizona Rangers were found with their throats cut from ear to ear."

Longarm shook his head. "That is bad news. And those boys are tough and well-trained fighters."

"That's right. And a federal marshal from Tucson was sent down to find out what was going on and he was later discovered stripped, tied to a wagon's wheel and burned to death. No one would have even been able to identify his body except that he carried a second tin shield that his murderers obviously overlooked. The officer had scratched his name on the back of his badge. It was blackened but clear enough to read."

"Was it someone I knew?"

23

Billy's fists clenched in his lap. "I'm afraid it was our old friend, Marshal Scotty Atkinson."

Longarm rocked back on his bare heels, then took a seat beside Billy on the couch. "Are you sure?"

"Positive."

Longarm slammed his fist down on the arm of the couch. "I told Scotty not to go down and work out of that Tucson office. That's rough country and there's even rougher men down along our southern border. But Scotty's wife had the rheumatism and the doctor said she'd be in a whole lot less pain in a hot, dry climate. I guess she just couldn't take our Colorado winters anymore."

"I know. Scotty deserved better than to be tortured and then burned alive."

Longarm could feel the bitter bile rising in his throat. Scotty had been one of his early mentors. A man who had been capable, fearless, smart and cautious. If someone had trapped Scotty, then they must have been exceptionally clever.

"So what's going on now?"

"I got this telegram yesterday," Billy said, removing it from his coat pocket. "It's from Tucson asking for our help."

"Why us?"

"Because Scotty was our friend and because they've already lost too many men to send more. I was thinking about sending Marshals Jasper and Clark."

Longarm shook his head. "Whoever was smart enough to kill those Arizona Rangers and then Scotty is smart enough to eliminate Jasper and Clark. They wouldn't stand a chance down there."

"I know it and you know it, but they've volunteered."

"Tell them thanks but no thanks."

"If I do that, who can I send?" Billy asked, avoiding Longarm's eyes.

"I guess we both know the answer to that one. I'll have to go."

"But you're wounded," Billy protested but not very forcefully. "And you've been on a tough case."

"There's no choice," Longarm said. "Scotty was our friend and he was a part of our team for too many years to let his murder pass without trying to bring the killers to justice. But I don't quite see what this all has to do with the Killion family."

"Brendon Killion was shot to death not a mile from where Scotty was found. There were hoofprints and enough signs to read that whoever murdered Scotty had been badly wounded and had ridden onto the Black Scorpion Ranch."

"Did the authorities follow the tracks to the headquarters?" Longarm asked.

"No."

"Why the hell not?"

"Because they were ambushed and forced to turn back." Billy sighed. "Three days later, word leaked out that the family's only son, Johnny Killion, had died and was buried in the ranch's cemetery."

"Hmmm," Longarm mused. "Scotty must have shot both Johnny and his father before he was captured and burned."

"That's the way it looks. The authorities down there are running scared. They didn't dare go out to the ranch. However, when Brendon's widow and his two daughters came into town for supplies a few days later, the local marshal tried to question them about the killings."

"And?"

"And they were greeted with silence. The rumor now is that the widow is planning to pay Mexican bandits fifty thousand dollars to come back across the border and wipe the town of Spur off the map and declare that its ruins belong to Mexico."

"That's crazy!" Longarm spat. "The United States government would send troops down there and quickly end the matter."

"I'm sure they would," Billy agreed. "But that would spark a war between us and Mexico. Right now, Mexico is on the verge of having another revolution. Hundreds, maybe thousands of people would die and many more would suffer. We think that it would be far better to avoid open confrontation with the powers that are now fighting for the control of Northern Mexico."

"So this trouble needs to be handled without the interference of either our government or that of Mexico?"

"Exactly. That's what I was in meetings about yesterday. The word is that neither government will become engaged. That only individuals will settle the matter and they are to do it quietly and without fanfare. We don't want the newspapers to be swarming around down there asking questions. This is a very deadly and delicate situation."

"Sounds to me like whoever is behind all this has thought it all out."

"I agree. And our main suspect has to be Mrs. Veronica Killion. She now controls her late husband's ranching empire, and I don't have to tell you how much money she can spend in order to see that her aims are met."

"I'll leave on the train first thing tomorrow."

Billy stepped around behind Longarm and studied the heavy bandage on his shoulder. "How bad is your wound?"

"Just a scratch," Longarm replied. "Won't slow me down one bit."

Billy looked suspicious. "Are you sure?"

"I'm standing here, aren't I?"

"Yes, but you look worn and pale."

Longarm heard a sneeze from under his bed and realized he needed to get rid of his boss fast. "I didn't sleep all that well last night. I'll be better tonight. Why don't you let me catch another couple of hours of sleep and we can have lunch and talk over the details of this mess down by Mexico."

"Did Miss Baker greet you at the train station?"

"As a matter of fact she did."

"Where is she?"

"Beats me."

Billy glanced into Longarm's bedroom and his eyes narrowed behind the lenses of his spectacles. "Custis, have you suddenly started wearing dresses and women's undergarments?"

"Of course not!"

"Then maybe you had a visitor last night."

"Look, Billy," Longarm said, trying to grab his boss and steer him toward the front door. "I'll get shaved and dressed and come on over to the office. We can go to lunch and you can give me all the details about this case."

"I've already told you what little I know. Dead Arizona Rangers and then the terrible news about Scotty. Furthermore, I expect that Veronica Killion and her daughters are behind these murders. From what I've heard, the whole family was drunk with power and ambition. The Killion women wear guns on their hips and I understand they can outdraw and shoot almost any man. They are supposed to be beautiful but as deadly as a den of rattlers."

"I've had to arrest women before."

"None like those vipers."

Longarm didn't have anything to say about that when Audrey began a fit of violent sneezing.

"Who's under that bed?"

"No one you need to see."

"Custis, you look like hell and now I'm beginning to suspect why. You needed rest and instead, you picked up some woman in a saloon and . . ."

"He didn't pick me up in a saloon," the voice said as

it cleared its throat. "You sent me to meet him at the train, remember?"

"Audrey?"

She stuck her head out from under the bed. "Hi, Mr. Vail. I'm sorry to hear about all the trouble. But you also need to know that Marshal Long really isn't up to going out again so soon. His shoulder is bad and he probably needs to see a doctor."

Billy looked at Longarm. "Is that true?"

"No. I'm fine."

"He isn't!" Audrey insisted. "The man needs rest and medical attention. Do you want to lose him?"

"Of course not." Billy shook his head. "Miss Baker, uh, why don't you just stay and take care of Custis until he is ready to return to duty. Help him along. All right?"

"Sure, as long as you don't tell the office how you found me under Custis's bed."

"Of course I won't. But you were the one woman that I thought could be trusted to do the right thing."

"She did do the right thing," Longarm said. "Now get out of here. I'll see a doctor and come by later."

"Okay," Billy said, glancing back through the bedroom door at Audrey. He shook his head again and muttered, "My god, what have you done to the poor girl?"

"Nothing that she didn't want done," Longarm assured his boss as he practically pushed him out of the room.

When the door was closed, Audrey crawled back out from under the bed and wailed, "Custis, I'm ruined!"

"No, you're not. Billy is far too much of a gentleman to tell what he saw just now."

"Are you certain?"

"Yep."

Audrey expelled a deep breath. "That may be so but after this little humiliation, I'm not eager to look him in the eye again."

"It'll pass," Longarm told the woman. "How about some coffee and breakfast?"

"I'll get dressed and we'll go out to eat and then you'll see a doctor about that shoulder."

"Fine," Longarm told her as he went to collect his clothes.

Chapter 4

Two days later, Dr. Carl Mason nodded his head in satisfaction. "That shoulder is healing nicely," he said. "Young lady, I suspect that you are the one largely responsible for the marshal's speedy recovery."

"I like to think so," Audrey replied, "but, as you can see, the man is almost indestructible. He has the constitution of a horse."

"And the instincts of a stallion," the doctor said, blushing slightly. "Or at least, that is the rumor we hear at the office."

"Don't believe it," Longarm said, shrugging back into his shirt. "Doc, I have to go down to the Arizona border with Mexico. I should have gone two days ago."

"If you had," Mason said, "you'd have suffered a setback. As it is, you've no business leaving so quickly. The wound has scabbed over nicely but, if you were forced to exert yourself, it could open up again and you couldn't stand to lose a great deal more blood. We weighed you again today and you're still fifteen pounds under what I would consider to be your ideal weight."

"Thanks to Miss Baker's cooking, I've put on five pounds in two days," Longarm said. "She's quite remarkable in the kitchen." Longarm could have added that she was equally remarkable in bed but he didn't want to embarrass Audrey.

"When do you need to leave?" the doctor asked.

"Tomorrow morning."

"I don't advise it," Mason said. "But I know that you're going to do what you have to do. After all, I've been your doctor for at least five years and you've never once taken my medical advice seriously. I heal you . . . you go out on some assignment and return in terrible shape . . . then I heal you again and the cycle repeats itself."

"Don't think I don't listen to you or appreciate your advice."

"Oh," Mason said, "I'm sure you do appreciate it, but you ignore it all the same."

"I think I should go with him," Audrey said. "I think he needs my help."

The doctor looked to Longarm who slowly buttoned his shirt before he said, "Doc, I'd like to take Miss Baker, but it would be too dangerous. I've explained that to her a dozen times but she refuses to listen. Will you please tell her that I'm serious?"

The doctor, a widower in his mid-thirties with a prematurely graying beard and kind, but sad, eyes, turned to Audrey. "I'm sure that you want to do the right thing and help the marshal, but I've seen him long enough to know that when he says something is dangerous. He's most likely even understating the situation. Miss Baker, taking care of Custis Long is difficult and challenging enough. I sure don't want to see any serious harm or injury befall you."

"But you can see how much I've helped in his recovery."

"Yes, I can," Mason said, "but he would have recovered rather quickly under his own devices. Please, Miss Baker, I strongly suggest that you go back to whatever job or pastime you have and let the marshal do his job without the added concern of your welfare."

"I don't like my job," she told him. "And besides, I'm sure that I'd be the topic of malicious gossip concerning my role helping Custis."

"You have medical talent and experience," Mason said. "I know at least three Denver doctors who would love to hire you as an assistant."

"You do?" Audrey brightened.

"Of course! But I'm only going to tell you the name of one doctor because he is by far the nicest but overworked."

"What's his name?"

"Why it is *my* name, of course."

"You need an assistant?"

"I certainly do. So when can you start to work?"

Audrey turned to Custis. "Are you sure that you'll be all right and not do anything stupid or reckless? Dr. Mason isn't exaggerating when he says that you couldn't stand the blood loss of either another wound or the reopening of that shoulder."

"I promise."

"And you'll come back to us?"

"I'll come here even before I go back to my apartment."

Audrey nodded her head and turned to Dr. Mason. "In that case, I'll accept your job offer starting tomorrow morning after Custis's train departs."

"Excellent!" Mason was grinning and his eyes had suddenly lost their normal sadness. "I'll start you at forty dollars a month. I . . . I expect you might have been making more with the government but . . ."

"Forty dollars is fine," Audrey said, looking almost as happy as the doctor. "It *is* less than I was earning and I will have to find a more inexpensive apartment, but that's fine."

"Now that you've got mine all cleaned, you can stay

there until I return and save yourself some rent money," Longarm told her.

"That would be wonderful."

So it was settled. That night Longarm, Audrey and Dr. Mason, who had sort of invited himself, went out to a wonderful dinner and had a good time. Later, Longarm had to practically shove the doctor out the door of his apartment. They'd had a few brandies and Carl had proved to be quite the raconteur, funny and witty but with a very definite sense of humor that was self-deprecating.

"He's a nice man," Longarm said when the doctor was finally gone. "I think you'll like working for him very much."

"I'm sure that I will. I'll miss Mr. Vail, however. But I think he would have always been a little disappointed in my morals and been embarrassed by my presence, as I would have been in his presence."

"Billy is puritanical but he understands life," Longarm told her. "And I know he'll be sad to see you quit. But I think that Dr. Mason really needs someone not only to help him in his office but also to be a friend and a comfort."

"Yes. I suppose. But you don't think that he has any designs on me, do you?"

"Naw," Longarm lied because he'd seen right from the start that Dr. Mason had been completely enchanted with Audrey. Longarm had never seen the normally shy and often melancholy physician so animated. Audrey's presence had affected him like a rare and rejuvenating medicinal tonic. "I'm sure that he does appreciate your beauty, but he'd have to be blind to do otherwise."

Audrey's eyes misted. "I told you before that you were blunt and certainly no poet but, Custis, there are times when you say things that make a woman's heart melt like butter."

"And I just said one of those things?" he asked with a smile.

"You sure did." Audrey reached for his belt and soon, they were back in bed, Longarm sinking deep into her lush and lovely body.

It was drizzling and cold the next morning when Longarm went to the train station with Audrey and their mood matched the dismal weather. Their good-bye was quick and sealed with a long, passionate kiss followed by a few rushed words of farewell.

Longarm hated good-byes, especially with women he had loved. So he boarded the train and tried not to look down at the platform where she stood huddled in the wet weather. None too soon, the train was moving and he was reading the morning newspaper, not really aware of what he was reading. He had a strong hunch that Audrey Baker would mourn his leaving, but then find happiness and satisfaction working in medicine. He also had a very good feeling that, in a rather short time, she would discover that Dr. Carl Mason was a wonderful man and would make an exceptionally loving husband.

"I hope it works," Longarm said to himself, "even though it would have been nice to have come back home to her again."

With that thought and his blessings for the pair, Longarm closed his weary eyes. He and Audrey had not slept very much last night. Their lovemaking had been frequent and powerful. Longarm was very tired and he was glad for the opportunity to sleep. It would take him at least five days to reach Spur, Arizona. In that time, he would try to sleep as much as possible and also to eat as much as possible, both of which he'd promised his doctor and Audrey.

"Excuse me," a soft, very feminine voice said. "Can you tell me where I might find the conductor?"

Longarm roused himself and turned to see a cute little blonde standing with her head poked into his private compartment. "You can't find the conductor?"

"No. It seems that there has been some mistake."

"What do you mean?"

"I mean that I'm ticketed for this compartment."

Longarm's eyebrows raised. "Is that a fact?"

"Yes." She entered the small space whose plush seats could be made up into a nice-sized bed. "Here is my ticket," she told him as she extended it forward. "As you can see, I am supposed to be in compartment number seventeen. *This* compartment."

Longarm reached into his vest pocket and extracted his own ticket. He scowled and then shook his head. "My mistake. I'm very sorry. I'm in the next compartment."

He got up to collect his bag and coat. "Oh," she said, "you don't have to jump up and rush off just yet."

"I don't?"

"No, of course not. I'm . . . well, frankly I'd appreciate someone to talk to."

"I see."

"Yes. You see, I only came to Denver the day before yesterday at the request of an old friend. Well, he isn't actually old. We had met several years ago in New Haven, Connecticut, when I was visiting my brother while he was attending Yale to study law."

"You don't say!"

"I do say. Douglas was my brother's closest friend. I wasn't especially taken with him when we first met but . . ." The blonde smiled and blushed slightly. "I did know that Mr. Douglas Johnson, Jr., was quite a catch and rich as anything."

"Quite rich, huh?"

"Oh, very! His father was a snobbish and very successful New York lawyer. My brother told me that Douglas was quite a blade but, actually, he was really a

36

monstrous bore. Oh, but I must be boring you with my chatter."

"Not at all," Longarm said quickly. "Actually, I'm fascinated by your story."

"Good. Anyway, I came here to see Douglas. He'd broken up with his fiancée and his letter to me was desperate, so I came. But it was a mistake. I mean, he's going back to New York City mostly to be near his mother, whom I understand is a horrible old biddy."

"What a shame," Longarm said with mock sympathy.

"Her name is Agatha and he talks about her all the time. Well, I just couldn't stand it more than a day and a night. Ooops! I shouldn't have told you that, I suppose."

"Sit down," Longarm said. "Would you like a little shot of good whiskey for a cold, wet morning?"

"I'd love a shot of your whiskey."

"It's the least I can do for mistakenly taking your compartment. Now, tell me more about this Douglas Johnson."

"He's now an attorney, just like my brother who lives and practices in Tucson. But they couldn't be more different! Anyway, it didn't take me long to get away from boring old Douglas. So now I'm heading home. And by the way, where are you going?"

"I'm going to a little town called Spur."

"I know where it is, but have never been there. What is your business, if I may ask?"

"I'm a Deputy United States marshal."

Her fingertips flew to her rosebud lips. "Why, that's what I guessed you'd be the minute my eyes saw you on the passenger platform. And was that your lovely wife saying good-bye?"

"No, just a friend."

"A very good friend, judging from the way you said good-bye. But I shouldn't have said that either."

Longarm was amused and interested. "You can say

37

whatever comes to your mind," he told her as he found his silver flask and poured the young woman a capful.

She raised the cap of whiskey and saluted him. "I'll bet you're anything but boring."

"That's not for me to judge," he said modestly. "But I have had a few adventures in my line of work."

"I'll just bet you have." She tossed down the whiskey, shuddered, then giggled. "That is good stuff. I'm not acting much like a lady, but I think it's important to have a little whiskey on such a foul morning."

"I couldn't agree more." Longarm took a drink and smiled. So far, they hadn't even told each other their names. Not that it mattered. Longarm knew that they would get to know names and a whole lot more about each other before they finally reached Tucson.

So much for catching up on the rest and sleep, he thought, feeling the little man begin to reawaken and come to life in his pants.

Chapter 5

The long, usually difficult and dangerous journey to Tucson, Arizona, had proven to be far more enjoyable than Longarm could have ever hoped. And now, as he and Julie Miller neared that old southwestern desert town, they were having one last sample of each other in the rocking stagecoach they had boarded after leaving the train. Longarm had mounted Julie who was pinned against the heavy upholstery. The potholes and bumpy road made his thrusting deep, varied and, if Julie's reaction was to be taken as evidence, highly satisfactory.

"Oh Custis," she moaned, shapely legs locked around his waist. "It's a good thing that we're almost at the end of this trip or you'd kill me with that big thing!"

"You want me to stop?"

"No! Keep it up all the way into town!"

He laughed. "I don't think that would be a very good idea. You probably have a sterling reputation in Tucson that I don't want to ruin."

Julie nipped his earlobe and sighed with pleasure. "I don't care what people think. I just want you to promise me that you'll come back when that nasty business down at Spur is finished."

Longarm knew that he could not hold back more than a few additional thrusts. And then, suddenly, the coach hit an especially deep pothole and he impaled Julie who screamed.

"You all right?" he asked with concern.

"Oh yes! Custis, it felt like you were coming up through my throat that time."

"Not hardly," he grunted, resuming his pumping until Julie's pleasure-glazed eyes rolled up and her mouth flew open with a scream of ecstasy. "Oh yes, my darling! Yes!"

"Hey!" the stagecoach driver up in the box shouted. "You two better finish it up quick because we're coming into town!"

Longarm gazed out the window and saw that the driver was right. The coach rounded the end of Main Street and then began to slow. Longarm's lips pulled back from his teeth and he moaned as he spewed the very last of his seed into Julie's sweet honey pot. For a moment, they held each other in a sweaty, locked embrace and then Longarm rolled off the small but energetic woman.

"Oh my," Julie said, pulling on her underclothes and trying to quickly get herself presentable. "I'm so wet between my legs that I just know I'm going to be leaking something terrible when we stop."

"Hold your legs tight together until you can get somewhere private to clean yourself up," Longarm advised, jerking up his own pants and noting with some dismay that they were also wet and sticky with Julie's warm juices. "I got a coat in my bag that would cover up my pants but it'd look pretty fishy given that it must be a hundred degrees outside."

"I'm not only leaking," Julie wailed with consternation as she tried to keep her legs tight together, "but I'm covered with sweat and my dress is all wrinkled!"

"It happens. I hope that your brother isn't going to notice."

"How could he fail to notice?" Julie tried to compose herself. "If he sees me in this condition, he might decide to kill us both!"

Longarm frowned. The last thing he wanted to do was to have to fight Julie's brother or cause a big stir that would bring embarrassment to this passionate young woman.

"Driver!" he shouted. "Stop the coach!"

"Marshal Long, it's still two blocks to the livery."

"I don't care. Stop it right now!" Longarm demanded.

The driver drew his sweaty team of horses to a premature stop outside of the first saloon in town. Longarm gave Julie a quick kiss, then said, "I'll be looking you up when we're both presentable. That way, your brother won't try to kill me."

"Thank you!" she breathed, still trying to wipe herself dry.

"Comb your hair and button up your dress," Longarm advised as he jumped down with his satchel, then shouted up at the driver for his bag. "Driver, if I hear any stories about what you imagine went down in this coach, I'll be looking you up and arresting you for . . . for defamation of character."

"Fer what?"

"Never you mind," Longarm warned. "Just keep your lips buttoned up about Miss Miller or you'll find yourself in a whole bunch of trouble."

"Yes, sir!" the driver said. "I didn't see nothin'. Didn't hear nothin' either."

"That's the idea," Longarm said with approval as he tossed the man up a silver dollar.

"Thank you kindly!"

"Drive a little slow the rest of the way. Miss Miller isn't quite ready to present herself."

"Not surprisin'," the driver said with a knowing wink.

41

"But mum is my word and you can pin your star on that, Marshal."

"Good."

Longarm shut the door but not before grinning at Julie and saying, "If your brother asks why you're all sweaty and smelly, just tell him you petted the horses at the last stage stop and they slobbered all over you."

Julie made a face. "Custis, even my brother knows that horses don't smell like what I got leaking between my legs."

"Then tell him there was a randy dog that didn't have any manners and that he tried to mount you. Tell your brother that someone shot the dog for insulting your honor and that it was such a humiliating experience you don't want to talk about it."

"Good idea." Julie blew him a kiss and began to frantically comb her hair as Longarm grabbed his bag and satchel, then headed for the saloon for a beer.

The sun was ferocious. It was well over a hundred and the idea of being down in this hot country trying to solve four murders and prevent a border revolution sure wasn't anything to feel happy about. Longarm glanced down at his soiled pants and hurried on into the saloon. It would be dark there and he'd sip a few beers and see what he could find out about the Killion family and their Black Scorpion Ranch while Julie's sweet juices dried on his trousers. In this brutal heat, he didn't think that should take long.

"Good afternoon," the bartender said in greeting as Longarm came through the door. "It's a real pisser out there, ain't it?"

"Yep."

The bartender had only two other customers, both sleepy-eyed Mexicans who looked like they were either very drunk or bored to death. Taking up a dishrag, he selected a glass and polished it to a dull shine. "Beer or whiskey?"

"Whiskey," Longarm replied. "As long as it isn't rotgut."

The bartender was a congenial looking man in his mid-thirties. Of average height, he had long, stringy black hair and when he moved, Longarm could see that he was making only a half-hearted attempt to hide the fact that he was missing both ears.

Not wanting to stare, Longarm turned and glanced at the two Mexicans, then said, "Not much excitement today, huh?"

"Oh," the bartender answered, "it gets pretty busy at night. Couple more hours, the men will start drifting in, and they'll be thirsty after such a hot day."

"I expect so," Longarm said.

"Haven't I seen you before?" the bartender asked, studying Longarm with real interest.

"Maybe. I've been in Tucson a couple of times."

"You're . . . you're a lawman, ain't you?"

Longarm always preferred to keep his identity and his business private, but the worst thing an officer of the law could do was to be caught in a lie. "I am."

"I expect you're here because of what happened last month with them Arizona Rangers and that federal marshal gettin' murdered."

"You're a sharp one, aren't you?" Longarm drawled.

"Well, I am for a fact," the bartender said, missing the sarcasm. "You know, we've been talking about them murders and I been tellin' everyone that the law would come around again. How many officers did the government send this time?"

"Just between you and me?" Longarm asked, lowering his voice in a confidential tone.

"Sure. I understand you fellas don't always wanna show your hand. Not right away."

Longarm looked the bartender right in the eye. "What if I told you that I was the only one that was sent to investigate those murders and bring the killers to justice?"

The bartender poured a full shot of whiskey and winked. "Why, I'd say that I believed you, Marshal. Of course, we both know that ain't true."

"Mister," Longarm said, raising his glass, "there's just no foolin' you and that's a fact."

"I am a very intelligent man," the bartender agreed, so pleased by the compliment that he poured a shot for himself. He raised his glass to Longarm and said, "We'll just keep it our little secret."

"Let's do that," Longarm said, matching the toast and knowing that the bartender would be telling everyone in Tucson tonight that there were a whole bunch of United States marshals in town, but that this important news was to be kept a secret.

They drank two more rounds and the bartender said, "I expect that you've noticed that I'm missing both ears."

"I noticed."

"Furthermore, I expect you, being a lawman, are real curious as to how I lost 'em both."

Longarm wasn't curious at all. On the frontier, a missing ear or two was a fairly common sight. In a bad brawl, men often bit off their opponent's ears. "I guess I am," he said, not wishing to disappoint the bartender.

The bartender grinned as if he were about to share a great treasure. "The fact is, Marshal, that the great Apache Chief Geronimo cut 'em off and fed 'em to his dogs."

"No kidding?"

"I swear it on my Irish mother's grave! You could ask anyone around here and they'd say George Harvey got his ears cut off by Geronimo so he could feed his dogs. And then you'd probably want to know why Geronimo didn't cut off my head or slit my throat."

"I would."

"Well," Harvey said, leaning across the bar and drawing back his long, greasy hair so that Longarm could fully
appreciate how close his ears had been shaved off, "the
truth is that I was so brave that Geronimo decided to spare
my life. Yes, sir! Because I didn't flinch, nor howl nor
nothin' when he cut off my ears. I just stood there in front
of that Apache and his friends as solid and strong as a
cigar store wooden Indian. Geronimo looked me in the
eyes and saw that I had no fear."

"I'll be dogged," Longarm said, trying to look as if he
believed the man and was tremendously impressed.
"That's really something."

"I was always brave," the bartender confessed. "I was
an Indian fighter before the years and the rheumatism
forced me behind this bar, which I own. I don't mind
being a bartender much, but sometimes the conversation
gets pretty stupid and dull. But then again, someone like
yourself comes along that I can see is as intelligent as
myself and it all seems worthwhile."

"Tell me what you know about the murder of the Arizona Rangers and federal Marshal Scotty Atkinson."

"Well," Harvey said, "first you have to remember that
Spur is about seventy miles to the south of us. It ain't
much of a town, so most of the people down along the
border come up here to buy their supplies and groceries."

"Is Spur just a little ranching settlement?"

"Yeah. There's nothing except a couple of saloons and
a livery. There's a lot of horse and cattle trading back and
forth across the border and none of it is legal."

"So you see quite a bit of the Killion people and their
cowboys?" Longarm asked.

"We do. The Black Scorpion Ranch is one of the big-
gest spreads in southern Arizona. They run cattle and
horses all over the country between Spur and Tucson. Old
Brendon Killion, he either shot, bought or run off anyone
that homesteaded this country before he arrived, so now

he has laid claim to more land than any one family has a right to own."

"Tell me about the trouble," Longarm said.

"Well, Marshal, it was clear that there was big trouble brewing down here for years. You see, Old Brendon was way too friendly with the Mexicans and he was running stolen guns, cattle and horses back and forth across the border. When he wanted to sell them, he'd gather up his boys and they'd come storming up the road into our town. He used to come in here at least twice a month and get drunk. He'd buy drinks on the house until the cock crowed in early morning, and I can tell you that he saw himself as being pretty important among the Mexicans."

"I understand that his son, Johnny, was also killed at about the same time as the lawmen."

"That's right. Johnny was as wild and as hard as his father. The town of Spur and Tucson are better off with both of them Killion men dead."

"Who do you think shot them?"

"Marshal Scott Atkinson was the one. The Arizona Rangers got ambushed before they had a chance to kill or arrest anybody. It was a sad deal, I'll tell you."

"So did anyone see the killings?"

The bartender shook his head. "Not to my knowledge. And, if they did, they're either dead now or else they're smart enough to keep quiet about it."

Longarm nodded. "I understand that the widow, Mrs. Veronica Killion, is deep in mourning."

"I wouldn't know about that. She rarely comes up here to visit us in Tucson. She prefers to shop down in Mexico. But when she needs supplies, she allows her two daughters to be escorted up to this town once or twice a month. I can say one thing for a fact."

"And that is?"

"That Mrs. Veronica Killion is ageless. She looks nearly as good as her daughters and they're the prettiest things that anyone in this country ever set their eyes upon. But they're all deadly."

"Who told you so?"

"Marshal, I once saw Mrs. Killion gun down a man who dared to look at her ankles when she lifted her skirts to keep 'em out of the mud."

"She gunned the man down for that?"

"That's right," Harvey said. "However, to her credit, she did give the cowboy a chance to get down on his knees and beg her forgiveness. It was Sunday afternoon and everyone was watching. This cowboy, he'd had a few drinks and you could tell he was scared, but he wouldn't apologize. So Mrs. Killion drew her six-gun and shot him dead on the street. Three bullets in the heart, so close together you'd think they was only one bullet that punched his ticket."

Longarm was accustomed to hearing stories about gunfights, but this one caught him a bit off guard. "And there were plenty of witnesses?"

"At least a dozen or so of us. Right after that, Brendon Killion appeared and he was so proud of his wife that he picked her up in his arms, carried her into my saloon and they stayed until they were too drunk to walk. It was quite a celebration."

"How old are the Killion daughters?"

Harvey poured them both another shot of whiskey. "Let's see. I'd guess that Gloria is about twenty-five. Her sister, Zona, is only a year or two younger. They're like twins and you can't hardly tell them apart. Both are dark-eyed beauties like their mother and many a young man has made the mistake of thinking he had a chance of courtin' 'em but . . . well, never mind."

Longarm sensed that Harvey had been about to reveal something important. "If you got something I need to know, then say it."

Harvey cast a quick glance at his two sleepy-eyed Mexican customers, then leaned close and whispered, "The rumor is that those daughters are anything but virgins. It's just that they are real careful in who they sleep with. Some say that they belong to General Escobar and his lieutenants."

"And he would be?"

"Escobar is the one that was secretly in cahoots with Mr. Killion. He's the man that is trying to form an army big enough to reclaim the southern part of our territory. I don't know it for sure, but I've heard that he is the man that Mrs. Killion is helping."

"I see."

"I've never seen the general, but I have seen a few of his soldiers. They're rough-looking sons of bitches. Slit your throat and mine for the price of a beer."

"Does General Escobar ever cross the border?" Longarm asked.

"I wouldn't know about that. I don't even know what he looks like," Harvey confessed. "Some say he's a real big man with one of his own ears sliced off. Others say he's a small fella who was born of a noble Spanish family that was thrown out of power. That he only lives for revenge and is deadly. That he lives to kill and is crazed by the lust for power . . . like Brendon Killion used to be. I just don't know."

Longarm nodded with understanding. "Well," he said, "I'd better think about how I'm going to get down to Spur."

"You could catch a ride on a wagon," the bartender suggested. "There are at least a couple going and coming every day. Or, you could buy or rent a horse and ride on down there. But I wouldn't advise either."

"Why not?"

" 'Cause the minute them people in Spur know that you're another federal marshal, you're a dead man."

"Maybe I'll take along some help."

Harvey nodded. "You mean other marshals."

"That's right."

"You could do that. But you know what I'd suggest?"

"No. Tell me."

"My advice would be for you to just wait until the Killion clan comes up here to Tucson. They're due to arrive any day now. Up here, you got a better chance of having your own way. But down on the border you're at their mercy."

Longarm nodded, understanding the logic. "Maybe I'll just take your advice. Who is the local marshal here in Tucson?"

"His name is Elias Ring and he's worthless," Harvey said. "He is in cahoots with the Killions all the way. Ring talks a good line, but don't trust the man. Hell, Marshal, half the officials on our city council are indebted to the Killion family in one way or another."

"Thanks for the warning," Longarm said, preparing to leave.

"Come back anytime," the bartender called. "I never get out of this place unless it's to run over to the red-light district for a few minutes of pure pleasure."

As Longarm turned to make his exit, he was surprised to see that the pair of sleepy-eyed Mexicans were gone. They'd slipped out so quietly, and he'd been so absorbed in what George Harvey had to say, that their absence was completely unexpected . . . and troubling.

"Hey, Marshal!"

Longarm paused at the door and turned. "Yeah?"

"Keep your partners close and watch your back."

"I will," Longarm vowed as he headed out into the sun-blasted street.

Chapter 6

Longarm was tired and decided that he needed to get a room and at least spend one night in Tucson. Tomorrow, clear-headed and rested, he could decide what to do next. George Harvey's advice made sense in that it might be wiser to wait and face the Killion family right here in Tucson rather than down in Spur.

As he walked downtown, he again became aware of just how old and venerable Tucson was. A Catholic Church near the presidio had a sign telling one and all that it had been founded by Spain in December of 1775 and named San Agustin del Tucson on the east bank of the Santa Cruz River.

Longarm was well aware that the early Spaniards and Mexicans who founded the town had been long-suffering at the hands of the fierce Apache. It wasn't until the Gadsden Purchase in 1855, which added southern Arizona to the Union, that silver mines had been discovered and the little Sonoran Desert town had began to flourish. Then came the Civil War and the Army had abandoned its garrisons leaving the citizenry once again to the mercy of the Apache. For nearly a decade, Tucson had been a town under constant siege.

"Good afternoon!" the clerk at the Ocotillo Hotel said. "You'd be United States Marshal Custis Long. Welcome back to Tucson and my hotel."

"News travels fast," Longarm said, trying to recall if he'd met this friendly hotel owner before. "I need a room."

"And a bath, I imagine," the man said as he turned the hotel register toward Longarm for his signature. "Riding the stage is a hard and dusty way to travel. But things will change when the Southern Pacific Railroad arrives. Won't be too long now."

"I'll be glad of that."

"Yes, sir," the clerk said, "there is nothing like the arrival of a railroad to bring prosperity to a town. Why, I'm sure that the real estate values in Tucson will one day be the highest in the entire Arizona Territory. And when we finally win statehood, then things will really start buzzing in this neck of the woods."

Longarm didn't bother to tell the man that the woods in this country were damn few and far between. Instead, he signed his name and said, "The last time I stayed here, I paid fifty cents with a bath included."

"Had to raise my rate to sixty cents a day. Help isn't as cheap as it used to be. You look like you could use a laundry for your suit. Want me to take care of that?"

"I'd appreciate it," Longarm said.

"Sorry about having to raise the room rate, but my costs keep going up every year. In January, I had to replace the roof and I'll tell you that cost plenty."

"I'm sure it did," Longarm said. "The last time I visited, I had a room that gave me entry either to this lobby or to the back door. That worked out just fine."

"You had lucky room number seven. And judging from what I've heard about you coming here to solve those murders . . . I'd say you need all the luck you can muster."

"I suppose that I do." Longarm took his key. "Is the little cafe just a couple of doors down the street still good?"

"They serve the best steaks in town and their pies are outstanding. Say, Marshal?"

Longarm turned. "Yeah?"

"Are you aware that we are under threat of invasion from south of the border?"

"That's what I've heard. Apparently there's a trouble-maker down in Mexico named General Escobar."

"That's right. The infamous and mysterious General Miguel Hernandez Escobar. Of course, no one has ever seen the man and survived, which only makes his legend all the larger."

"I understand that General Escobar and Brendon Killion were close friends."

"Both men were infected by the cancer of ambition. Mr. Killion could have been contented to be rich and powerful given the size of his ranch holdings, but that wasn't nearly enough. He yearned for political power, or so I'm told, and sought it through the favors of General Escobar."

"What did he expect to get from a Mexican invasion of southern Arizona?"

"Unlimited power like a king would have in Old England. All I know is that his widow and his daughters are also friendly with the general and his officers."

"I see."

"Marshal, if you go down to Spur and start nosing around, they'll kill you," the hotel man warned.

"That's what I've heard. And I've no authority south of the border."

"Then I don't see what good you can do. The government should have sent an army instead of a dozen of their best federal marshals."

Longarm had no idea where this man had gotten the "dozen" number, but it sounded impressive. "Well, I'm tired, dirty and I'm ready for a bath," he said.

"Very good. And if any of the other marshals that are here incognito want to stay, I do have a number of rooms still vacant."

"I'll tell 'em."

"Thanks. Business has been pretty slow. Many of us are just trying to hang on through this miserable summer. The last thing we need is some damned so-called Mexican general stirring things up and getting us bad attention all over this country. That kind of publicity will kill our real estate market. Maybe there's some way you could just sneak down south of the border, ambush the general and nip this whole revolution thing in the bud before it has a chance to snowball out of control."

"Are you serious?"

"Of course I am! Couldn't you just shoot the general from cover, then hightail it back across the border?"

"That's not the way a federal marshal does business. I'm not an assassin."

"Well," the clerk said, "maybe you ought to change the way you think, so we can put all this revolution talk behind us. I'm telling you, Tucson can't stand grief from Mexico in addition to all the Apache trouble. You and the other marshals are going to have to act fast and be decisive. Brendon Killion is dead and I say good riddance. Now, all you have to do is kill General Escobar and accept our gratitude. That ought to be straightforward enough."

"It is."

"And don't forget about my vacancies."

"Not a chance."

Longarm went to his room and took a bath. A China-man arrived at his door to take his clothes for cleaning and damned if the man didn't wrinkle his nose when he

54

smelled the lovemaking juices. He grinned but didn't say a word.

Longarm shaved and then took a nap waking up about six o'clock to the sound of a knock at his door. Figuring it was the Chinaman returning with his laundry, but not willing to take any chances, he reached for his revolver. "Come on in!"

A handsome young man in a three-piece suit appeared. When he saw Longarm in the tub with a gun pointed in his direction, he threw up his hands and cried, "Don't shoot!"

"Who are you?"

The man hooked a forefinger under his collar and took a deep breath. He was sweating heavily and looked very nervous. "I'm Julie's brother. Oswald P. Miller, Esquire."

Longarm reholstered his gun. Oswald was thin with a black moustache and a goatee. About six foot tall, he looked rather delicate and scholarly and did not appear to be armed.

Longarm frowned. "Mr. Miller, as you can plainly see, I'm taking a bath. What do you want?"

"I'd like a few words with you, but I can wait in the lobby for however long it takes you to become presentable."

"Speak your piece," Longarm ordered. "I expect your business concerns me and your sister."

"Julie spoke quite glowingly of you, sir. And I'm very glad that she was in your company."

"You are?"

"Of course. The Apache still attack stagecoaches in Southern Arizona and I was relieved to learn that you were with Julie while she was crossing the most dangerous parts of our territory."

Longarm relaxed. Apparently, Julie had managed not to raise her brother's suspicions. "So what do you want?"

"To invite you to dinner this evening."

All Longarm wanted was to have a quiet meal at the cafe and then retire early. "I thank you very much, but some other evening when I am more rested."

"I expected you to say that. Julie will be disappointed, of course, but I'll tell her that you will favor us with your company some other time."

"Thanks."

Longarm watched the young lawyer fidget for a moment and knew that there was something else on Oswald's mind. Finally, the attorney asked, "Marshal, may I take a seat?"

"Sure. You've got something to say. Out with it."

Oswald laced his fingers in his lap. "The simple truth is that I very much want to help you bring the murderers to justice."

"Are you serious?"

Oswald nodded vigorously. "I have never been more serious of anything."

"Why?"

"Among other things, Marshal Atkinson once saved my life. And because I came to look upon him like the father that Julie and I should have had. Scott Atkinson not only saved my life, but he was my hero. He was past his prime to be a lawman in a rough town like this, but still brave and totally honest. He couldn't be bribed and he couldn't be bought . . . though I suspect that Brendon Killion tried hard to do both."

"Did Scotty tell you that?"

"Yes. And I won't rest until you arrest the man or men that murdered him from ambush and I have convinced a jury to send whoever is guilty to the hanging tree."

Longarm didn't miss the passion in the lawyer's voice but he quickly dismissed the idea of Oswald being of any real assistance. "You said, 'Among other things,' " Long-arm commented. "What does that mean?"

"It's not important."

"I'll decide that."

Oswald got up and began to pace back and forth across the floor. Finally, he blurted, "Quite a few years ago, I was deeply in love with a young lady who lived near Tucson. We had planned to be married."

"What happened?"

"She was abducted."

Longarm frowned. "By the Apache?"

"Everyone in town thought so at first. She had been traveling with her parents in a buckboard. It was attacked about forty miles south of town. Both her parents were . . . were tortured and killed. Natalie was never found. Only later did I learn that she had most likely fallen into the hands of the Mexican revolutionaries."

"Exactly how long ago was this?"

"Seven years," Oswald choked. "I'm twenty-eight. Natalie would be twenty-five."

Longarm could see the anguish on the young man's face and wanted to say something that might help ease his pain. "Maybe it turned out all right for her. Maybe your Natalie was treated kindly."

Oswald shook his head. "Don't try to make me feel better at the expense of truth, Marshal. She was kidnapped by killers. Those kinds of people would have used her for their pleasure and probably, when there was little left of her . . . put an end to Natalie's life."

"Was she a white woman?"

"Yes. Why do you ask?"

"What color hair did she have?"

"Reddish-blond. Her hair was the color of maple syrup. She was very, very beautiful. And I'm not the only one who thought so. Everyone in town did. Natalie was special."

"Then she was probably spared the worst of what you are imagining and sold to someone with wealth. That's the way it often happens south of the border."

"Marshal Atkinson tried to convince me of that, but I never really believed him."

Longarm shrugged. "Some people like to punish their minds by always thinking the worst. I'm not saying that your Natalie didn't suffer a terrible fate and is dead . . . I'm just telling you that she *might* have survived down in Mexico."

Oswald was inconsolable. "But even if she had, what kind of a life would she have lived? And wouldn't she have been forced to marry against her will?"

"I can't say," Longarm replied. "But who knows? You can think the worst . . . or the best. It's your choice. Why not think it turned out all right for her and let it go at that."

"Because I just can't." Oswald groaned. "You know, I have never even been with a woman. I never wanted any other woman than my Natalie."

Longarm was not sure that he understood. "Are you saying that you're a . . . a virgin at twenty-eight?"

He nodded.

Longarm shook his head in complete and utter amazement. "Man, you don't know what you've been missing. Oswald, are you sure that you even *like* women?"

The lawyer blushed. "If you're asking me if I am . . . odd . . . well, I'm not. Julie would tell you the same. I'm not, for instance, attracted to you even though you are virile and handsome."

The conversation was making Longarm a bit uneasy. Uneasy enough that he didn't want to climb out of the tub just yet. "Well," he said, clearing his throat, "I guess we've hashed that over well enough and this bathwater

58

is getting cold. Been nice talking to you, Oswald, and I'll be happy to come over for dinner sometime in the future, if all goes as well as I hope."

"But I want to help on this case! I am prepared to risk my life to bring Marshal Atkinson's killers to a swift justice."

"I'll keep that in mind."

"No, you won't," the man said, voice rising in anger. "I can read your face and you think I'd be worthless on a manhunt. You are convinced that I'd be *worse* than worthless."

"I didn't say that."

"Marshal, you don't have to say anything. You might be surprised to know that Marshal Atkinson taught me how to ride a horse and shoot a gun. He taught me a few things about tracking a man and surviving in a gun duel."

"He did?"

"Yes. I'm an expert marksman with rifle or pistol." A measure of pride filled the lawyer's voice. "No disrespect, but I became a better marksman than Marshal Atkinson."

"Better maybe at *target* shooting," Longarm said. "Not better in a gunfight."

"How would I know, having never had to draw a weapon on another human being?"

"Oswald, I believe you are a good man and probably a good attorney."

He puffed up a little. "I'm an *excellent* lawyer. I studied three years under Judge Goodman and two years under Judge Thomas. They both said I was the brightest and most talented law student they ever apprenticed."

"That's fine. Then what you should do is to continue practicing the law and let me do the job that I was sent to do."

"How many other marshals did the government send?"

Longarm wanted to tell him a lie that would get him

the hell out of the room but that didn't seem to work so he said, "I'm the only one."

Oswald slapped his forehead with the palm of his hand. "Oh my goodness! You can't be serious?"

"Afraid so."

"If that's true then you're a dead man!"

Longarm had heard enough from this earnest but outspoken fool. He stood and reached for a towel then dried himself off. "Listen," he told the lawyer, "I've been sent into situations that should have gotten me killed more times than I can even remember. But I always survived. And I'll survive this time on my own."

"Do you know that the Killion women will make sure that you don't even get across the border alive? That their men will see you in Spur and you'll be targeted for an ambusher's bullet?"

"Maybe I'll figure out something on the way down," Longarm said, knowing his words sounded lame.

"And maybe you need someone that Mrs. Veronica Killion trusts and who can get you in and out of Spur alive."

"Who could do that?"

"I could," Oswald said. "I represented Johnny Killion more than once and kept him from going to prison."

"He was your friend?"

"In a way. We were complete opposites. He was wild and out of control. He and his father whored and frequently drank themselves into stupors here in Tucson. They fought and they were thoroughly disgusting."

"So why did rich and lawless Johnny Killion decide to be your friend?"

"I usually kept him out of jail. Even so, he at first delighted in tormenting me."

"So what changed him so that he became your friend."

"You may not believe this because I know I don't look fierce or strong but, when he pushed me past my limit, I struck Johnny with a uppercut that dropped him dazed to the floor."

Longarm was impressed. "You knocked down a Killion and lived to tell about it?"

"Yes, I did. Johnny jumped up and challenged me to a fight. So we fought to a draw. You see, Marshal Atkinson had also taught me a thing or two about fisticuffs."

"Scotty was a tough man in a fight."

"You bet he was. I saw him whip many a larger man and I kept after him until he showed me how to protect myself against bullies. I daresay that I could even give a man like yourself a good scrap if I were pushed to my physical limits."

"Well," Longarm said, "I'm not going to do that. I've got more than enough trouble ahead of me already. So finish telling me about Johnny Killion."

"There's not much else to say. After I held my own against him with my fists, he vowed he would shoot me dead and that's when Marshal Atkinson showed him a tin can that I had riddled with a six-gun at fifty paces. Five bullets dead center."

"And Johnny Killion believed that it was *you* that riddled the tin can?"

"Not quite. But I could tell he was worried when he challenged me to a target shoot at one dollar a bullet. We made a bean can dance all the way up a hillside and when the shooting was done, Johnny Killion knew I was the better man with a pistol."

"Well, I'll be damned," Longarm said, finally believing the lawyer. "I would never have guessed it."

"I became proficient with weapons so that one day I could go down into Mexico and rescue Natalie . . . if she still wanted to be rescued."

"Oswald, I'm impressed by your dedication but I'm still not taking you to either Spur or Mexico."

"You need to change your mind."

"Why is that?"

"Because," Oswald said, "you won't win without me and I can't do what I must without you. And that, I swear, is the awful truth. And you do have the authority to deputize me, don't you?"

"I could do that," Longarm admitted. "But I would have to write out a letter saying that you are prepared to risk your life and would hold nobody but yourself responsible for injury or even death."

"I'm the lawyer. I could write that out."

"I'd prefer to do it myself."

"Does that mean that you will take me with you tomorrow?"

Longarm dressed slowly, his mind on this dilemma. He didn't want Oswald's help and yet, he was pretty sure that the earnest lawyer would follow him if his offer was refused. And why not accept help? It was clear that Oswald was still in love with his childhood sweetheart and would never be at peace until he'd at least made the attempt to find and rescue the girl. A girl that was most likely dead.

"Well, Marshal?"

"All right," Longarm said. "I'll deputize you."

"Splendid!" Oswald was all smiles.

"But only after you sign my letter saying that neither I nor our federal government bears any responsibility for what might happen when we ride south."

"I understand. Do you have an extra badge I can wear?"

"No."

Oswald tried to hide his disappointment. "That's all right. Just so long as I have the letter and the authority of a deputized lawman."

"And one other thing," Longarm said. "First thing tomorrow morning we'll walk out to the edge of town and I'll see if you're really the marksman that you say you are."

"Not a problem, only Tucson is big. Why don't we ride horses?"

"I don't have a horse yet."

"I have two. Both of them are strong, surefooted and fast."

"Saddles?"

"One for each of us. And I didn't see a rifle with you or in this room. You're going to need one."

"I know that. And provisions."

"I can get us a discount at the general store."

Longarm strapped his gun on and reached for his hat. "Why don't we go find something to eat down at the cafe and make a few plans even though you seem to think you have everything already worked out."

"I'd like that. But why spend the money when Julie has a good beef roast in the oven and is anxious to see you?"

"Does she know that you came here not only to invite me to dinner but also to try and talk your way into having me deputize you?"

"Of course she does."

"And?"

Oswald shrugged. "She's worried. I won't try to tell you that she's very much against my plan to find Natalie. She thinks it's a fool's errand."

"I'm afraid that your sister is probably right."

"I don't care," the lawyer said stubbornly. "I'd never be able to live with myself if I didn't at least try to find Natalie. I can't shake the idea that she is not only alive, but saving herself for me."

Longarm shook his head. "You may be smart and good with your fists and your guns, but you are very naive."

"Not really. I'm not that old yet but I have already seen the worst in men. I've seen the darkness that can corrode the human heart and cause it to do unspeakable injustices. None of that matters."

"Then what does matter?"

"Only that we follow our own true course in this life. Live honorably and do the best that we can. Never shirk our duty and never compromise our principles. Like Don Quixote."

"Like who?" Longarm asked.

"Like a man that lived a long time ago and who titled his lance at windmills."

"Why'd he do something dumb like that?"

"Because his honor demanded he do so."

"If he wrecked the windmill, it wouldn't pump water," Longarm said, not impressed. "And any man that would wreck a working windmill would have to be considered ha lunatic."

"Don Quixote might have been a little on the crazy side but he was not so different from you, or Scotty or perhaps . . . I'd like to think . . . even myself. He was a man who had a true heart and lived with his own code of honor."

"If he'd have wrecked a homesteader's windmill in eastern Colorado where water is often in short supply, I'd have had to arrest the poor fool. And why in the devil did he do it with a lance?"

"Never mind, Marshal Long. Let's go get something to eat and then you can come to my office and write out the letter for me to sign. And as for a badge, I'll find one by tomorrow morning."

"What about the local marshal?" Longarm asked. "I usually find it important to let them know what I'm doing in their town."

"Marshal Ring is incompetent and worse," Oswald assured him. "The best thing we could do is to avoid him completely."

Longarm remembered he'd heard the same opinion before and nodded in agreement. He would sidestep Marshal

Ring and tomorrow they would head for Spur. But tonight, he might just manage to maneuver Julie into a real bed when her brother went to his own lonely bed dreaming of the ghost of a girl named Natalie.

Chapter 7

It was almost ten o'clock and Longarm was getting ready to head back to his hotel. "Julie," he said, "you cook a mighty fine dinner. I can't thank you enough."

"Must you leave?"

"I should. Your brother is in the next room and I don't want him to get upset."

"And I'm afraid that he would," Julie confessed as she followed Longarm out to the little front porch. "Oswald is such an idealist. I expect he thinks that I'm as pure as the driven snow. A virgin just like himself."

"Well," Longarm said, "let's just let him believe what he wants to believe. You know, I'm not too keen on the idea of his coming with me to Spur and then possibly into Mexico."

"Neither am I." Julie sighed. "Oswald may have told you that our mother died when we were quite young and our father was a drunk who terrorized both our lives. My brother and I grew very close early on and he is my dearest and best friend. If something bad should befall him . . ."

"I understand. But what can I do? He is obsessed with finding Natalie and I am sure that he would go down into

Mexico searching for his childhood sweetheart even if I refused to allow him to accompany me as a deputy."

"He would," Julie agreed.

"Then I have no more choice in the matter than he does," Longarm said. "Is he really a marksman or was that just talk so that I'd agree to deputize him?"

"Oswald is deceiving to the eye," Julie said, linking her arm with his and leading Longarm to a porch swing where they could sit and rock. "I know he looks . . . well, quite harmless. Even weak. But Oswald is a fighter at heart. And he is an expert marksman."

"He said that Scotty . . . Marshal Atkinson . . . taught him how to use his fists and to track a man down."

"That's also the truth. They were like father and son. My brother remains infatuated with the memory of a girl that is now most likely dead. He also carries the burden of our marshal's loss. That's why he is so thin. He doesn't eat and I know that he sleeps poorly. For a time, his interest in the law kept him on an even keel, but I fear that he is now close to going over the edge."

"So you're telling me that Oswald is a little unstable?"

"I'm telling you that, unless he avenges the death of Marshal Atkinson and he at least learns the truth about what happened to his childhood sweetheart, my brother will always be a man haunted by the ghosts of his past."

Longarm cracked his knuckles. "Oswald said that he is welcome at the Black Scorpion Ranch. That Mrs. Killion likes and trusts him enough that he might be able to get me into Spur and Mexico."

Julie's face hardened. "I love my brother, but I wish he had never met the Killions. He and Johnny became friends although they could not be more different. I think that Veronica Killion would like to seduce my brother."

"Really?"

"Yes. With the possible exception of the youngest daughter, Zona, that whole family is evil. You must protect my brother from Mrs. Killion and her oldest daughter, Gloria. And you must protect yourself from those two women. I can't tell you how cunning and immoral they both are. They would do anything to preserve their power and get a man under their spell."

"They're really that bad?"

"Yes," Julie said. "And also that dangerous. Many a young man has fallen under their evil spell and come to a terrible end. Be very careful for they are beautiful and spellbinding witches."

Longarm laughed nervously. "I take it that you don't like them."

"I despise them! They have weaved their web of entrapment even up here into Tucson. Marshal Elias Ring is under their power. He's little more than their puppet and whenever Johnny or his father would get into trouble here in Tucson, they had Ring to protect them from any justice."

"Have you ever been to Spur?"

"Oh yes. Several times. It's a bad border town. It's lawless and filled with border scum. In Spur, you'll find the worst of the worst." Julie snuggled up close to him. "I would give anything if you and Oswald didn't have to go down there tomorrow."

"Me, too. But it's my job and I couldn't leave without bringing my friend's murderer to justice."

"Come back safe," Julie said, her voice filled with anxiety. "If I lost you both down there . . ."

"You won't," Longarm promised.

Julie raised her head and kissed him with desperate urgency. "I want you one more time."

"What about your brother who doesn't sleep very well?"

She squeezed his hand. "We have corrals and a hay barn out behind the house."

"You want me to make love to you in the hay?"

"Why not?"

Longarm grinned. "Sure," he said, coming to his feet, "why not?"

It was almost midnight when Longarm finished with Julie. Grunting and thrusting, he emptied his sack with the last of his seed, then stood and pulled on his pants. Julie lay bathed in the soft yellow light of a kerosene lamp that hung on a nail.

"Thank you," she said quietly. "Maybe after what you just did to me I can sleep tonight after all."

"I sure will," Longarm replied, stifling a yawn as he shoved his feet into his boots, then reached for his gunbelt. "Good night, Julie."

"Good night Marshal Custis Long. And may God protect you and my dear brother and bring you both back safely to my arms."

"I don't kill easy," Longarm said. "And I'll do everything in my power to protect Oswald."

"Who knows," she said, "he may be the one who protects *you*."

"Maybe," Longarm said a moment before he put his hat on his head, brushed the hay off his clothes and headed back to the Ocotillo Hotel.

Longarm was up and out of his room early the next morning. He returned to the cafe for breakfast and was enjoying his meal when a tall, heavyset and unshaven man in his early forties stormed through the doorway, looked over the crowd and then said, "Are you another gawdamned federal marshal they sent from Denver?"

Every eye turned to stare at Longarm who answered, "I am a deputy United States marshal. And you'd be Marshal Elias Ring."

"That's right, mister. And we're going to have us a little talk right now."

"Fine," Longarm told the irate lawman. "Sit down and have yourself a cup of coffee while we talk. I was just finishing my breakfast."

"You are finished," Ring spat. "We'll talk over at my office like we should have done yesterday when you and Miss Miller got off the damned stage."

Longarm took a sip of his coffee. He had seen far too many jealous and threatened local lawman in his career and Elias Ring was just the last of an often incompetent bunch afraid that they would be upstaged by an intruder with federal authority. He made one last effort to diffuse Ring's anger.

"Why don't you sit down and quit shouting? We can talk in your office just as soon as I'm finished with my coffee and I've paid my bill."

But Ring reached into his pocket and then hurled a handful of coins on the floor. "You are finished right now, mister! Follow me!"

Longarm couldn't believe his ears. Despite all the unflattering comments he'd already heard about Elias Ring, he was still not prepared for the man's anger or uncivilized behavior. Everyone in the cafe was still staring, wondering what Longarm would do next.

He remained seated, sipping his coffee and reading the day-old copy of the local Tucson newspaper.

"You probably ought to do what Marshal Ring says," a man said. "Ring can be pretty rough when he's crossed."

"Your marshal doesn't know what rough means," Longarm said, drawing a cheroot from his vest pocket and biting off its tip before poking it between his teeth and searching for a match.

The same man found a light and held it out to Longarm, who saw that his hand had a slight tremor. Longarm puffed contentedly and said, "Relax. This has nothing to do with you."

"I guess it don't," the man said. "Uh-oh, here he comes again!"

Ring came storming over. He didn't stop at the counter but blew past it and came to a halt next to Longarm's window side table. "Are you damned hard of hearing?" he shouted.

Longarm smiled and shook his head back and forth. His obvious lack of concern further infuriated the local lawman, causing him to snap. When Ring's hand shot out to grab and yank Longarm out of his chair, all hell broke loose. Longarm hurled the contents of his coffee cup into Ring's eyes and when the man cried out with pain, Longarm stood up and punched him square in the face. Ring staggered, wiped the hot coffee from his eyes and charged.

Longarm dodged the onrush and Ring, still half-blinded, went crashing through the window in a shower of broken glass.

"My window!" the proprietor cried. "Oh no!"

"Don't worry," Longarm said, teeth still clamped on his cigar as he strode past, "your marshal will pay for it."

Ring was dazed and bleeding from a dozen or more lacerations to his ugly face as well as his neck, arms and hands. When Longarm reached the man, he grabbed and hauled him to his feet, spied a horse watering trough and dragged Ring over to it tossed him into the trough.

And even then he wasn't finished. He took a fistful of the man's hair and shoved his head under water, holding it for more than a minute while Ring went crazy with terror.

"Are you ready to pay for that man's window you broke and to show a fellow lawman some respect?"

Ring shook his head so Longarm shoved it down again and, this time, he held it even longer.

"You're going to drown him."

Longarm glanced sideways and saw that it was Oswald. "Someone should have done it already."

"I'd have to try you for murder if you succeed. And neither of us wants that, do we?"

"No, I guess not," Longarm reluctantly agreed as he allowed Ring's head to resurface. "But he needs to pay that cafe owner for his window."

"That is debatable since you threw him through the window."

"I did not! He ran through it and I barely touched him." Longarm dragged the man out of the water and searched his pockets until he came up with a few dollars in cash. Then he hurled Ring into the dirt. The thoroughly beaten man scuttled away like a crab.

"I'm going to pay the man for his window and then I think we'd better get ourselves provisioned for the journey south."

"Good idea," Oswald said, finally breaking into a wide smile as Marshal Ring disappeared behind a building.

Chapter 8

Late afternoon the next day, Longarm and Oswald passed a ramshackle farmhouse. Suddenly, three immense mongrels raced toward them, barking and growling as if they were going to tear the legs off the horses. Longarm could see an old man standing on the porch of the house and the man didn't say a word as his dogs charged up the lane to intercept the passing horsemen.

"Dammit, call them off!" Longarm yelled.

But the man either didn't hear the warning or else he thought he'd seen something quite interesting because he remained still and silent.

"What are we going to do?" Oswald asked as the trio of vicious dogs grew closer.

"Let's put some distance between us and them!" Longarm shouted, spurring the ugly buckskin that he was riding into a hard run.

Two of the dogs soon gave up the chase but the largest, a massive gray and white beast with saliva dripping from its chops, cut across a field and intercepted them.

"Look out!" Oswald yelled as the beast nailed the buckskin on the right rear hock and set it into a fit of wild bucking.

Longarm was a good horsemen but he wasn't a bronc buster and his horse quickly unloaded him. He struck a rock and was momentarily dazed. The next thing he knew, the huge dog was on him trying to tear out his throat.

Dazed and already bloodied by the fall, Longarm lashed out with his hands and then tried to protect his throat and face. He wanted to reach for his side arm but didn't dare expose himself to the animal's terrible white fangs.

"Oswald, shoot him!" Longarm bellowed.

An instant later, a pair of closely spaced shots rang out. The ferocious beast yelped then it dropped on Longarm's chest, jaws still working even as the life in its feverish yellow eyes grew dim. Longarm threw off the crazed mongrel and rolled to his knees. His right coat sleeve was in tatters and when he wiped his face with the back of his hand he saw blood.

"How bad are you hurt?" Oswald asked, jumping off his horse and kneeling beside Longarm.

"Bad enough. That was pretty good shooting. I'm glad that you killed the dog and not me."

"I hope he didn't have rabies."

"Me, too. Never saw a dog just come at a man or horse that way." Longarm twisted around and stared back at the ranch house. "That old son of a bitch is still standing there watching, isn't he?"

"Yes."

Longarm seethed with anger. "Let's catch up that jug-headed buckskin and then go pay him a visit."

Oswald helped him to his feet. "If we go back, there are still two dogs left."

"If they come at us again then it'll be my turn to show you some fancy shooting. Catch up our horses."

The buckskin didn't really want to be caught and by the time it wearied of its little game, they were another mile from the homestead and Longarm was feeling even worse.

Oswald studied him closely. "You don't look so good."

"I don't feel so good either. You ride the buckskin, I'll ride that sorrel gelding."

"All right, but I don't like the buckskin much," Oswald admitted. "I bought him after he won a horse race. He isn't much to look at and he doesn't have any manners, but he sure is fast."

"Fast to throw a man," Longarm groused as he hauled his battered carcass up into the saddle. "Now let's go have a word or two with that homesteader. He's going to pay me for my coat or I'll take it out of his hide."

"You don't look like you could do much hiding or anything else right now," Oswald said.

"Come on!" Longarm growled as he reined the sorrel around and they headed for the homestead.

When the old man saw them returning, he set his dogs at them again but this time Longarm and Oswald were ready. They shot both the animals in the head and that was the end of that menace. When the homesteader saw his dogs go down, he spun and disappeared inside his dilapidated house. A moment later, he appeared with a buffalo rifle.

"Holy cow!" Oswald shouted. "He's going to try and kill us!"

"Doesn't surprise me," Longarm said as the man raised the huge fifty caliber rifle. "And he's got the range on us so let's ride!"

Without another word, he reined his horse around and made a hurried escape back up the lane.

Moments later, Oswald and the ugly buckskin passed him as if he and the sorrel gelding were running in quicksand. When the buffalo rifle boomed, Oswald spurred hard and really put some distance between himself and Longarm.

A mile later, they reined in their horses beside a spring-fed pond and a large stand of cottonwoods. It was blazing hot and there wasn't a breath of a breeze. Longarm was feeling terrible and he dismounted, then handed his reins to Oswald and sat down with his back against a tree trunk. He felt weak and sick to his stomach.

"You going to be all right?" Oswald asked when he'd tied and unsaddled their sweaty horses.

"I just need to clean up and rest awhile. It's so damned hot we can wait out the worst of the afternoon right here in the shade of these big cottonwoods. I'll be ready to ride again come evening when the day cools off a bit."

"We've still got a considerable way to go before we finally reach Spur."

"How far is it to the Black Scorpion Ranch?"

"Maybe fifteen miles."

"That far?"

"I'm afraid so," Oswald replied. "And what about that old man that set his dogs against us, then tried to blow us out of our saddles?"

"I'll deal with him on the way back."

"*If* we come back."

Longarm removed his hat. "Don't worry about that. And when we do, there will be hell to pay for that old bastard."

"At least we proved we can shoot dogs."

If that was meant to be an attempt at humor, Longarm wasn't impressed. "I can shoot men, too, when I have no choice. But the real question is . . . can you shoot another man?"

"I could," the younger man insisted.

"We'll see," Longarm told him as he closed his eyes. "Get me some water from that spring. I want to clean up and take a nap."

"You look a lot worse than tired."

"Thanks."

Oswald found a rag and helped Longarm clean the blood off of himself. The fang marks on his arm and left hand were nasty-looking but not terribly deep, thanks to Longarm's efforts and his coat sleeve.

"Rest easy, Marshal. I'll stay awake and keep guard."

"Appreciate that," Longarm replied as he closed his eyes and immediately drifted off to sleep.

It was nearly dark when he awakened but it even seemed hotter. Longarm's eyes opened quickly and he stared at Oswald who said, "Marshal, I hate to say it, but you are running a high fever."

Longarm didn't argue the point. He felt as if he were on fire. "Maybe that dog did have rabies and I'm going to go crazy. If that's true, then you have to shoot me because there's no cure."

"I know that."

"Can you do it?"

Oswald looked away quickly. When he dragged his gaze back to Longarm, he gulped and said, "Marshal, I don't think I could shoot you like a rabid dog."

"It's a horrible way to die," Longarm told the lawyer. "I've seen animals die of it and I won't let that to happen to me. If necessary, I'll die by my own hand before I allow that to infect my brain."

Oswald peered through the fading light at Longarm. "You landed on your head and it's a miracle that your neck wasn't broken when you struck that big rock. I'm hoping that you've just had a mild concussion instead of contracting rabies."

"I guess we'll find out which it is before long."

"If I helped you into the saddle, could you stay upright until we reach the Black Scorpion?"

"I don't know."

"You'd never make it back to Tucson and Spur doesn't have a doctor, so we don't have many options other than the Black Scorpion."

Longarm managed a smile. "Everyone said that I'd be a dead man to cross onto that ranch."

"Maybe so, but I do have the favor of Mrs. Killion. I think it's our best chance to get you help. Marshal, you need more help than I can possibly offer."

"If I have rabies, not even God could save me. Help me up and let's get out of here."

Somehow, Oswald managed to get him upright, but that only showed Longarm how weak and unsteady he was on his feet. "Remember," he muttered, "I'm riding the sorrel and not your damned buckskin."

"I remember. I've saddled both horses. I'll bring them over. You just hold on to this tree and we'll soon have you in the saddle again."

Oswald was true to his word. And although he was slight, his appearance was deceiving, just as Julie had promised. When Longarm was in the saddle, Oswald mounted the buckskin and said, "I'll lead your horse. Just grab that saddlehorn and hang on tight."

The following hours passed in kind of a netherworld for Longarm. Feverish and with the heat of the desert clamped down hard against the land, his head swam and he drifted in and out of consciousness. It seemed like another lifetime when they finally stopped and he vaguely heard voices. The next thing Longarm knew, it was morning and he was in a bed staring up at one of the most striking women he had ever seen in his entire life.

"Good morning, Marshal Long," the woman with the dark eyes and long black hair said quietly as she leaned forward to wipe his brow with a cool, damp cloth. "How are you feeling?"

"I don't know yet."

She placed the cloth in a wash basin. "I am Veronica Killion and the mistress of this house. I am sorry that you have suffered so bad a journey down from Tucson."

"Where is Oswald?"

"In his room sleeping. It was very late when you arrived. He will wake up soon and then I'm sure that he will come in to see if you are still alive or dead."

Longarm reached up and laid the back of his hand against his forehead. "I feel somewhat cooler."

"You had a high fever last night, but you are very strong and it has already broken."

"Then I don't have rabies." It was a statement, not a question.

"No. But you do have a head injury. I don't know how bad it is, but it doesn't look good. We have sent for a doctor who lives just across the border in Mexico. I expect him to arrive at my ranch before noon."

"You are very kind."

"Not really," the woman frankly admitted. "But Oswald says that you are a good man and so we decided to see what could be done to help you regain your health. We wish you only the best and a speedy return to wherever it is you came from."

"Denver."

"Oh? All that way?" Her thick, arching eyebrows lifted as if she were impressed. "Then you must be very highly thought of among the federal bureaucrats in that city, which I have never had the pleasure to visit. How many more did they send beside you?"

"None. It's just me and newly deputized Oswald Miller."

"I don't believe you," she told him with a smile that held no warmth. "Already the federals have sent others and there is a question of the deaths of the Arizona Rangers. Very sad."

"I'm sure you grieve for them," Longarm deadpanned. "As you grieve for your late husband and your son."

Her eyes sparked and she warned, "Do not abuse my hospitality, Marshal. I will not tolerate sarcasm or bad manners. Especially not in the face of my generous hospitality."

"Sorry," he told her, realizing that he was in no position to antagonize the woman and that, at least for the time being, he was completely at her mercy.

Veronica Killion's eyes softened only a little and she rose to her feet saying, "I have other things to do. You rest and breakfast will be brought up to you soon. Can you eat?"

"I believe so."

"Good. We will talk more later."

It was on the tip of Longarm's tongue to again use sarcasm because he figured the only reason he was still alive was that this woman wanted to know exactly what she was up against from the federal government. But he clamped his jaw shut and nodded, trying to look grateful and submissive.

Instead, he probably just looked like a man who was badly bitten and battered. A temporarily helpless man smart enough to realize that time was now very much in his favor.

Chapter 9

Longarm's breakfast arrived on a tray carried by a plump Mexican cook and housekeeper who spoke no English. Longarm smiled, said, "*Gracias*, Senora," and enjoyed his breakfast. He was expecting Oswald to show up soon after he'd eaten, but the young man must have been very tired for he did not appear.

Instead, a dark-eyed young woman arrived to pick up his empty breakfast tray. Longarm knew at first glance that this beauty was not hired help but was one of the late Brendon Killion's daughters. The question was, which daughter? The older one that he had been warned was treacherous and whose name was Gloria, or the younger whose temperament might be kinder and who was named Zona?

"Good morning," she said without a smile.

"Good morning to you," Longarm replied. "My name is Custis Long."

"Yes. So Oswald told us last night. Deputy United States Marshal Custis Long, to be exact."

"That's right."

"You and some dog must have had quite a tussle.

You're pretty chewed up, so I'd say the dog got the best of the battle."

Longarm shrugged. "He was big and mean as a wolverine. I was lucky to keep him from tearing out my throat."

"Oswald feels terrible about that. He says that if you hadn't been riding the buckskin, it would have been him that would have been on the ground fighting for his life."

"I expect that's true enough."

She took his tray and placed it on a nearby writing table where he could still reach his coffee. Then, she took a seat in an overstuffed chair, leaned back and crossed her ankles.

"What none of us can understand is why you would come to our Black Scorpion Ranch. Surely you must have been warned that we were murderous people who had great plans to help General Escobar invade the southern Arizona Territory."

Longarm was surprised at her directness and decided to be just as direct rather than to feign ignorance. "Yes. I did hear those rumors while I visited Tucson."

"Well, then? Why did you come down into this country? Or, more to the point, why didn't you bring a company of soldiers?"

"I have no connection with the United States Army. I came down here to find out the truth. Sometimes, people make up the wildest rumors and blow things all out of proportion."

Her beautiful face did not reveal her reaction, but she asked, "Did you hear about the death of my father and my brother?"

"Yes, but without any details."

"Oh come on now, Marshal! Can't we be at least a little honest with each other? Surely you must have heard people say that my father and brother were behind the deaths of not only Marshal Atkinson, but also that of the Arizona

Rangers. Rangers sent down here already convinced that we are a family of liars, thieves, murderers . . . all plotting revolution and the overthrow of this territory."

"Zona, do you mind if I smoke?"

She was surprised. "How do you know that I'm not my sister, Gloria?"

"I have a sixth sense for these things," he said only half in jest. "I can usually figure out people. You fit the profile of the Zona that was described to me by people in Tucson . . . and by Oswald Miller."

She uncrossed her ankles and sat up, obviously interested. "Oswald described *me*?"

"That's right."

"And what, exactly, did he say?"

Longarm decided that he had better be flattering or the poor lawyer was going to be in deep trouble. "Oswald said that you were beautiful . . . but then I'd heard that all the Killion women were beautiful. But he was also of the opinion that you were the most easy to talk to and also the nicest."

"He said I was the nicest?"

"Yes. Oswald said you were as beautiful in spirit as you were in person."

This time, Longarm could see that he had said the right words because the young woman's expression softened and her eyes became warm, even a little misty. Clearly, she was infatuated with the young attorney from Tucson. Longarm decided this was going to work to his advantage if there was treachery in the minds of her mother and older sister.

"Did Oswald say other things about me?"

"He said you had an excellent sense of humor and a great appreciation for books and works of art. He said you were very intelligent and sensitive, but also possessed a strong will."

Zona beamed. "My! And I had not realized that Oswald knew that much about me."

"Well, he does," Longarm said, wanting to get the conversation moving into safer territory. "Zona, it's clear that he holds you in very high regard."

"Perhaps too high," she said, more to herself than to Longarm. "You can't live your entire life on a ranch in one of the hardest parts of the country without becoming somewhat hardened. Life is cruel out here in this dry, desert country. I have witnessed much suffering and death in my short life."

"Yes, and I'm sure that the losses of your father and Johnny were the cruelest."

Longarm expected Zona to agree and perhaps even show great sadness and emotion at the mention of those deaths, but she did not. Instead, she quickly changed the subject back to Oswald.

"He is still in love with the memory of a girl he once knew," Zona said. "His precious, never-to-be-soiled Natalie. Oswald is a fool to hold on to what is no longer real."

"Meaning?"

"Meaning that, even if that girl is still alive, she will not be the same person that he remembers as having such innocence and beauty. She would be hard and well-used. I doubt that he would even recognize Natalie if she were to walk up and stare him in the face."

"Have you told him this?"

"Oh yes! And he even nodded his head in agreement. But what the mind can accept, the heart often cannot."

"So what do you think will happen?"

Zona shrugged her lovely shoulders as if she did not care, though it was obvious that she cared very much. "I really don't know. But I am glad that he has come with you. Are you both proposing to go down into Mexico?"

"I suppose," Longarm said. "Marshal Scott Atkinson

was my friend as well as Oswald's and we were very close. We are both committed to bringing Scotty's killer to justice."

Zona studied his face for a long moment. "What if I told you that my brother killed your friend?"

"Did he?"

"Yes," she said evenly. "Marshal Atkinson shot Father and then my brother ambushed and shot him. But the marshal managed to get a bullet into Johnny and he also died. So justice, in the law's eyes, is complete. What is there left for you to do here?"

Longarm chose his words carefully. "Even if what you say is true, I would need an eyewitness."

"Johnny returned to this ranch badly wounded. He told us what had happened."

"Told who?"

"My mother and my sister and me."

"Go on."

"We tended to Johnny, but the bullet fired by Marshal Atkinson was too deep to remove. After two days and nights of agony, my brother died in his bed. His body was taken out and buried beside that of my father. You can almost see them from your window. When you are ready, we will take you out and you can stand over their graves."

"And what would that do?"

"Nothing," Zona said. "But neither will your coming here and then going down into Mexico prove anything except that you are a fool bent on dying."

Longarm lit his cigar and smoked quietly. "What about the Arizona Rangers? Did your father and brother also kill them?"

"I don't know for certain, but I don't think so. My brother and my father were very secretive. They didn't share a lot with me or my sister."

"Who do you think killed them?"

"Maybe General Escobar or some of his soldiers." She

shrugged. "Who knows? Perhaps it was someone who ambushed them for their horses, saddles and money."

But Longarm shook his head. "These were seasoned Rangers. Tough men. They would not have been that easy to kill."

"It is always easy for people to die along our border. This is a violent and a lawless land. There are many men on both sides of the border who are good with guns. Maybe even better than you, Marshal Long. In this hard, desperate country you learn early how to fight and survive or else you die young."

"I have been told that the Killion women not only wear six-guns but also know how to use them."

"You have been told the truth. Would it surprise you to know that my mother has killed men?"

"No. Will she allow Oswald and me to go into Mexico?"

Zona was quiet for almost a full minute and then she said, "This is something I don't yet know."

"Why would she try to stop us?"

"Because she is afraid that, if you are also killed, the United States will send soldiers and that they will consider us the enemy and take our land, cattle and horses."

"I see. But the truth is, that would not happen."

"So you say, Marshal. But you do not know what would happen for sure if another federal officer were killed. You would be dead and, therefore, could offer no help or guarantees."

"I guess you're right."

"Of course I am. Down here, we do not trust anyone. Especially not officers of the law."

"Maybe the Killions have a reason not to trust lawmen."

"We do. And do you know what that reason is?"

"No. Tell me."

"We prefer to be our own law."

"You can't do that," Longarm told her. "Not in this country."

"We have been doing it for many years."

"That time is over," Longarm said bluntly. "And, if you and your family fail to recognize the fact, you will suffer the consequences."

Zona took the tray and started to leave the room but turned. "We do not trust the federal government. We think that it would find us guilty even without proof."

"Then you people do not steal horses, cattle and guns and move them back and forth across the border for your own personal gain at the expense of this territory?"

"Marshal Long, we do what we must to protect ourselves and what we own on this land. To be weak is to be vulnerable. To be vulnerable is to be destroyed."

After she was gone, Longarm lay in his bed smoking and drinking coffee as he reviewed all the things that he had just learned or guessed from the young woman's visit. First, he was inclined to agree that Miss Zona Killion, the youngest of the three women, was not evil. Rather, she was a young beauty who had no illusions about the character of either her late father or brother. She was tough, but also vulnerable, in respect to her infatuation with Oswald.

Did the attorney know that Zona Killion was attracted to him? Probably not. Oswald was also smart and he had a tough, resilient streak, but he was blinded by a childhood love named Natalie. So blinded that he could not see what even a stranger could see and that was that Zona felt love for him.

"How can I use this in our favor?" Longarm asked himself out loud. "How can this help us find out for certain who killed the Arizona Rangers, given that Zona did not just lie to me about her brother ambushing Scotty?

The more that Longarm thought about this question and reflected on Zona's visit, the more he became convinced that his friend, Scotty Atkinson, really had been ambushed by Johnny Killion. It made sense and Longarm had not gotten the impression that Zona was a skillful liar. He could be later proven wrong, of course, but he did not think that was very likely.

Oswald appeared in the doorway, looking tired but cheerful. "Good morning, Marshal."

"Good morning, Deputy," Longarm said as he returned the greeting. "How are you feeling?"

"Hungry. I understand that you've already had your breakfast."

"That's right. On a tray."

"You rate well," Oswald said, stifling a yawn. "I thought that you might be dead by this morning of rabies, but Mrs. Killion tells me you are on the mend. She examined your head wound last night and told us that you had suffered some damage. That's why she sent for the doctor down in Mexico. He will also want to look at those fang wounds. Some of them are deep."

"I'll be fit in a day or two."

"I expect so," Oswald agreed. "And then we can ride down into Mexico and look for Natalie."

"That's *not* why we're going."

"Right. I'm still half asleep. We're going to find out who did those killings and if there really is a revolution brewing down in Mexico. What I discover about Natalie is inconsequential."

"That's not entirely true. I want to help you find that girl . . . or at least to learn if she is still alive. But it has to be the secondary reason, not our primary reason for riding south of the border. Is that clearly understood?"

"Sure."

"I hope so," Longarm said. "Because, if you don't understand that, then we aren't riding together."

"I said that I understood."

Longarm studied the young man trying to determine if

he was being truthful. The last thing he wanted or needed was for Oswald to go off on his own quest for a long lost childhood sweetheart.

Dammit, he thought with irritation, *why do things always have to get so complicated?*

Chapter 10

"Oswald?"

Oswald turned suddenly to see Zona standing out on the veranda and, to his surprise, realized that she was motioning for him to come out and join her.

"Good morning," he said, feeling a little self-conscious because of her extraordinary beauty. "Going to be hot again today."

"This country is always hot."

"Oh, it's not so bad in the winter," Oswald reasoned, trying to sound optimistic despite the already intense morning heat. "We ought to feel lucky that we don't have to shovel snow or worry about blizzards."

Zona smiled. "I'd like to see snow some day and I'd prefer a blizzard now and then to our constant heat."

"You might think so, but you'd soon tire of freezing weather," Oswald told her. "I've never been up in Wyoming, Montana or the Dakotas, but I've talked with men who have been there and they say they'd take the heat over the cold any day."

Zona considered this for a moment. "Maybe that proves that we always want what we haven't got."

"I hadn't thought of it that way, but you could have

something there. But what would someone like you have left to want? I mean, you're already rich and beautiful."

"You think I'm beautiful?"

"You're the prettiest woman I've ever seen."

"But not as pretty as your Natalie." She knew instantly that she'd made a mistake when his cheeks turned crimson and said, "I'm sorry. I had no right to say that."

"It's all right." Oswald came over to stand beside her. "The truth is, I've sort of forgotten what Natalie even looked like. I recall the color of her hair and eyes but . . . well, beyond that, I'm not sure anymore other than she was also beautiful and good."

"I talked to Marshal Long this morning. He says that you're going down into Mexico together."

"That's right."

"Don't you realize that Mexico is very dangerous?"

"Sure. But we have to find out who murdered Marshal Atkinson and those Arizona Rangers."

"My brother shot Marshal Atkinson and was mortally wounded by him. I explained this to Marshal Long, but he said he needed an eyewitness. I told him there were none except my dead brother and father."

"What about the Arizona Rangers?"

She shrugged her shoulders. "No one knows who killed them. Maybe they were ambushed for their money and horses."

"I doubt that Marshal Long will accept that as a reason. I think that they were killed by General Escobar or his revolutionaries. We have to find out and bring them to justice."

But Zona shook her head in disagreement. "There is no justice south of the border. There is no justice even on this side of the border. My father was the law here and my brother would have taken his place as head of our family."

The young lawyer shrugged. "I better get some breakfast. The marshal says that he'll be ready to ride south tomorrow."

"Let him go by himself. If Marshal Long insists on dying, why suffer the same fate?"

"Because I have to go. If Marshal Long hadn't showed up, I'd have gone down to Mexico on my own."

"Oswald Miller, you are smart with books and the law, but outside of that you are a complete fool," Zona snapped. "You should go back to Tucson and grow old practicing law."

"I'm sorry you think I'm a fool. I guess that's the truth, but I have to help find out what happened to Natalie."

Zona turned and left him before he saw her tears.

"I'm sorry!"

"Don't be," Zona whispered bitterly as she hurried inside. "I'll not mourn the death of any more fools."

The moment Zona was inside, she ran into her sister, who caught her arm and held it firmly. "What is wrong?" Gloria Killion asked although she was quite sure she could guess.

"Nothing!"

"That's not true. Did the marshal upset you this morning?"

"No."

"Then it was Oswald."

Zona's voice cracked with exasperation and hopelessness. "He is smart and yet so stupid! Why can't Oswald understand that he will only go down into Mexico to die? That his death will be for nothing!"

Gloria Killion's voice was filled with contempt. "You should not care what happens to the Tucson lawyer. If you must cry . . . then do it over a *real* man."

Zona could not hide her sarcasm. "Like all the ones that you've made love to?"

Gloria's dark eyes flashed with anger. "Zona, you can be cruel. Even so, I forgive you."

"I have nothing to be forgiven for."

"Ha! Don't you remember what the priest said? That we are *all* sinners. Even you, my little sister. If nothing else, I forgive you for falling in love with an unworthy weakling. A man with nothing but law books and a foolish desire to find a girl that no longer exists. A man who prefers to love a childhood *illusion* rather than a woman."

Zona pulled her arm free. "Maybe Oswald is foolish. But he has a very good and kind heart. His love is pure and that is something that you will never understand. He is the best man I have ever met . . . better even than most priests."

Gloria fought to control her anger. "So you believe Oswald is a man without a single weakness?"

"I didn't say he was perfect."

"But almost," Gloria said with a half-frozen smile.

"Yes. Almost."

"Well, my unwise little sister, I think we shall see about that."

Zona knew that tone of voice and it sent a shiver down her spine.

"What do you mean?"

"I mean that many things can happen to a man when he steps out of his world and enters another where all his beliefs are challenged. Your Oswald is about to be tested by fire and he will face many temptations and dangers."

"What are you thinking?"

"Nothing," Gloria said innocently. "But I'm curious about what you will do when your gringo saint is found to have feet of clay."

Suddenly frightened by the hardness in her sister's voice, Zona quickly added, "I told him that he should stop loving a girl that he freely admits he can barely remember.

96

But he won't listen, and so I have already washed my hands of him forever."

Gloria laughed coldly. "I don't believe you. If your dear, innocent Oswald were to somehow return alive from Mexico, you would forgive the fool."

When Zona said nothing, Gloria left her sister, who badly needed to learn that all men were cut of the same inferior cloth. That they were weak . . . especially when it came to the flesh and they were selfish and greedy. And while the lesson might prove painful, little sister would recover and be far stronger.

Once she was out of hearing range, Gloria said to herself, "Oswald is weak and only a man. And tonight, I shall prove it to Zona."

"So," Mrs. Killion asked when she and Gloria were together, "what did you find out from Zona?"

"She is in love with the attorney from Tucson."

"We already knew that."

"Zona is convinced that Oswald is purer even than a priest."

Veronica Killion smirked. "Your sister is old enough to know better. It is time that she had a hard lesson and learned the truth about men."

"I was thinking the very same thing," Gloria said. "And that lesson will be tonight, because they leave tomorrow."

"I know what you intend to do and you have my permission, although your sister will be heartbroken."

"Broken things sometimes heal stronger. Besides, I have never had a virgin man before. I didn't think they even existed."

"You must make it look like it was *his* idea. Otherwise, your sister will never forgive you."

"I understand."

"Wine," Mrs. Killion said. "We will give both Marshal

Long and his young deputy all the wine that they can drink."

"Why try to get the marshal from Colorado drunk?" Gloria asked, not understanding.

But the reason quickly became clear when her mother lowered her eyelashes and smiled beguilingly. "There is no reason why you should be the only woman who enjoys a man tonight."

"Mother, am I to understand that you intend to sleep with the federal marshal?" Gloria asked.

"Why not? He is big and I find him very attractive. And don't you think it is only fair that a man should have a last night of love before he dies? Like one enjoys his last meal before marching to the gallows?"

"Do you plan to poison him?"

"Once the man from Denver is dead, we can have his body dumped south of the border. Someone will find it fifty miles from our ranch and that will be the end of Marshal Long."

"But won't that bring even more trouble?"

"Not to us."

"Then to General Escobar?"

Veronica nodded. "But he is doomed anyhow. His stupid ambition will soon get him killed either by the Mexican army or by our army. Either way, he is better off dead."

"But I thought he was our friend."

"He was."

Gloria nodded, not sure that she understood. "If the general dies, the revolution is over."

"It never stood a chance of succeeding," her mother insisted. "I told your father that again and again, but he wouldn't listen to me. He was as blinded by ambition and greed as Escobar. In the end, it was the cause of their failure."

"Who really killed my father?"

"Marshal Atkinson! You know that."

"I thought that too at first," Gloria said slowly. "But now . . . now I am beginning to wonder."

Her mother shook her head and reached out for Gloria's hand. "Your father was killed by the federal officer. The same one that killed your brother. But, before he died, Johnny was able to fatally wound Marshal Atkinson. That is all there is to that, so let it go, my girl."

"I have," she assured her mother, even as she thought that maybe the old federal marshal had not killed her father after all. That perhaps he had died . . . at her mother's hands? Gloria forced a smile and looked quickly away.

"My dear," Veronica said, "are you troubled by something we can talk about?"

"No."

"Then maybe you are just excited about having that Tucson virgin tonight. Is that it?"

Gloria pushed the idea of her mother having a part in her father's death aside and managed to laugh. "Yes, that is it. Why, mother dear, in the morning, we can compare notes about our conquests. It will be amusing."

"Remember this, you must not let your sister know of our plan. If she found out . . . well, it would be very hard for even her to forgive and forget."

But Gloria shook her head. "My sister is incapable of holding anything against anyone for very long."

"It is her curse."

"That's true," Gloria agreed with resignation. "If we died, Zona would lose this ranch because she is weak. Sometimes, I cannot even believe that she is my father's daughter."

With a look of perfect innocence and barely concealed mirth, Mrs. Killion answered, "And what makes you so sure that *either* one of you are your father's daughters?"

"Mother!"

Now, as her oldest daughter stood with her jaw hanging in shock, it was Veronica Killion's turn to laugh.

Chapter 11

The Killion women, Longarm and Oswald gathered early that evening in the immense dining room seated at a massive table of dark, intricately carved and polished wood imported from Madrid, Spain. First they enjoyed tequila mixed with the juice of fresh mangoes on ice. It was a combination that was both strong and tasty.

"Where on earth," Oswald exclaimed, smacking his lips in obvious delight, "did you find ice and mangoes in the Sonoran Desert!"

Veronica smiled graciously, pleased that the powerful drink was found so delicious by young Oswald. "The ice comes from the high mountains just fifty miles or so to the east. We have a deep cellar and it is packed with straw so that we can enjoy cold drinks all summer."

"I have never had anything finer," Oswald said. "A man could drink this every afternoon and almost enjoy our blistering summers."

"Wait until you taste the wines," Gloria said. "They come from Mexico's finest vineyards. Do you also like this drink, Marshal Long?"

"It is a little on the sweet side for my tastes."

"We can fix that." Gloria clapped her hands and when

one of the family's many helpers appeared, she whispered rapid Spanish into her ear.

The dark-eyed servant bowed to Longarm and took his drink away prompting him to inquire, "What did you tell her?"

"There is something else that I am sure you will find more to your liking," Gloria said. "It was my father's favorite before-dinner drink. Not sweet but not bitter either."

Longarm was curious. "What's it made of?"

"Many things . . . all delicious. Drink two glasses and it will make you begin to laugh."

Longarm wasn't sure he was in any mood to laugh. His animal bites were still painful and his head still ached, even though the doctor from Mexico had arrived and given him headache powders late that afternoon. He had moments of double vision and he was not at all sure that he should be drinking anything powerful. But, on the other hand, maybe it would be good for his throbbing head.

When the maid returned, she presented him with a tall glass filled with ice and a lime-green liquid. He tasted it and found it was very much to his liking.

Oswald looked on with interest. "What do you think?"

Longarm took another taste and smacked his lips. "Whatever you have in this glass ought to be found in every saloon. Mrs. Killion, you could patent this drink and make a fortune."

But the woman shook her head. "The ingredients are too expensive."

Oswald's curiosity got the better of him, "I wouldn't mind trying one of those myself, if it's not too much trouble."

"That would be a mistake," Gloria said too quickly.

"Why?"

"They do not mix well with your drink and you might suffer the consequences."

"Oh, I see," the lawyer said, clearly not seeing at all.

When the supper finally arrived, it was a richly flavored grouse with rice and vegetables. By that time, everyone had enjoyed several of the iced refreshments and the conversation was easy and filled with laughter. Longarm no longer felt his injuries and whatever had been put into his drink had given him an almost euphoric sense of well-being. He also felt rather stimulated and found himself thinking of how pleasurable it would be to make love to any of the Killion women. Veronica was seated right next to him and her perfume was almost as intoxicating as his drink.

The meal ended with an excellent glass of brandy and Longarm discovered that his head no longer ached but that his vision was a little out of focus and the room was slowly turning. Deciding that he needed to retire for the evening, he excused himself, unaware that his speech was a bit slurred.

The moment he laid down and closed his eyes Longarm knew that the lime-green drinks he'd been served had been laced with a drug even more powerful than peyote. His body felt light but his manhood became as hard as a rock. The world continued to spin and yet he no longer felt queasy. His fingers and toes tingled and he had strange visions of swirling lights. Through them he saw figures that he could not identify but looked to be beautiful women moving through a rainbow mist.

"Marshal Long," the woman of the house whispered, sliding in beside him, feeling soft and cool. "I hope you do not mind if I stay with you for a few minutes of mutual pleasure."

Longarm wanted to tell Mrs. Killion that he was feeling very strange and that he doubted that he could bring either of them much in the way of pleasure. But his lips and tongue felt numb and he couldn't seem to speak.

"Are you unwell, Marshal?" she asked as her fingers ran down his chest, then his hard stomach to caress his manhood. "Oh, but this feels *very* well."

Longarm tried to frame an answer but failed. He could not even lift his arms or open and close his fists. *What has she done to me? What in the hell is wrong?*

"You are such a big, strong man," Veronica said as she began to explore his body. "But now, you are completely helpless and at my mercy. What a shame ... or is it? Maybe we will see what strange sensations we both feel when making love."

Longarm experienced a rising sense of panic and, at the same time, a welling up inside of him of such intense desire that his fingers, toes and manhood began to burn.

"You feel very warm," the woman breathed, her tongue now laving his erection. "I think you must be burning up inside. Is this so?"

Knowing he couldn't speak, Longarm did manage to move his head up and down in agreement.

"I will cool the fire," she promised as she mounted him.

A deep groan escaped Longarm and he lay locked in some kind of insane paralysis. His mind seemed to bounce off the walls that moved in and out around him and Longarm was aware that the woman riding his manhood was also groaning.

"You are a big man," she hissed in his ear. "But oh so helpless now. I wonder what you are thinking as I use you like I have been used by men. But you can't tell me that, can you? Poor Marshal Custis Long. What will become of you when I weary of this pleasure?"

Longarm didn't want to even imagine because he knew that she meant to first use him up and then be the instrument of his destruction.

"Marshal, try hard to guess."

Longarm couldn't react. He knew that he was being used and hated it, but there was nothing he could do to stop this relentless and diabolical woman intent on her pleasure seeking. Hours passed as again and again she spat her incoherent curses and and shuddered in repeated spasms of ecstasy.

Their bodies became slick with perspiration. The beautiful widow Killion gripped him with her powerful thighs and her fingernails sank deep into his flesh until he bled. Each time she cried out, she bit his neck, his shoulder and his chest. Blood mixed with sweat and finally, Longarm felt his own body began to buck and he choked and gasped as he was finally able to empty his sack with his tortured seed.

"Oh, very good!" she crooned softly. "I didn't think any man could drink what you were given at the table and yet still be able to pass his essence into my body. You are the first and the last."

Longarm lay panting and gasping for air. Soon, the woman began to manipulate him so that he was again hard. "Marshal, before sunrise, I swear I will consume your mind and your body. When I am finished, you will be nothing more than shivering, bloody flesh."

She is going to kill me, he thought. *I have been drugged. This woman is evil and insane. I am as good as dead already.*

The widow was doing something he had never had done before to the lower reaches of his body. Longarm tried to stop whatever it was and he must have made a helpless sound deep in his throat because she began laugh.

"Marshal Long. Can you understand me still? Can you hear my words? I think you can. You belong to me now. Just as your friend, the virgin attorney, is now helpless. Two helpless men in two separate bedrooms. Each about to lose the thing that they hold most dear."

Longarm raged inwardly. It was chillingly obvious that

this demented demon was going to kill him. But what did she mean about Oswald? Maybe there was still some hope for his friend, who had not drunk any of the lime-green poison. But Longarm knew his end was near.

Oswald had also felt as if his world was out of balance when he went to bed soon after Longarm.

I drank too much and now I am paying for it, he thought, gripping the sides of his bed as he lay sweating in the airless room. *But it will pass. I have been drunk a few times before and it always passes. Just hold on and wait it out*.

And so he did hold on. As Oswald was finally drifting off to sleep, he tried to think of Natalie, but her image seemed more distant and elusive than ever before. Soon, he was sleeping and then . . . then he was suddenly wide awake with a woman on top of him.

"What . . ."

"Shhh!" Gloria hissed, taking his manhood into her mouth and sucking on it as if it were hard candy.

"No!" Oswald protested. "This can't be happening!"

But the woman was making it happen and before he quite knew how to react, she slid his manhood into the warmest, softest most wonderful cavity he could ever have imagined. And it felt *so* good when she began to move.

Oswald squirmed and his protests grew weaker. He was still dizzy from the drinks, but he knew what Gloria Killion was doing. She was taking what he had saved for his precious Natalie.

"Don't," he said, not meaning it. "Stop."

Gloria laughed and her tongue was now wet in his ear. Oswald moaned with pleasure and, despite himself, his hands found her taut buttocks and he was pulling Gloria tighter and tighter against his thrusting hips.

"So," she said, breath hot on his face, hair tumbling

down as their bodies moved in a unison so perfect that Oswald never wanted it to stop. "So was your long virgin wait a mistake?"

"Oh, yes," he panted.

Gloria raised herself until only the very tip of his manhood was shrouded by her sticky wetness. "I could stop right now. We could stop and you could still hold what you have been holding inside for so many years."

His head thrashed back and forth on his pillow and he thrust upward, impaling her to the hilt of his fleshy sword.

"No! I want you!"

Gloria pulled his face down to her breasts and told him to suckle her like a hungry baby and make hard love to her like a real man.

Oswald tried one last desperate time to remember his cherished Natalie. Failing, he cursed in the darkness. Like a wild beast he roared and then rolled the woman over and mounted her in a consuming frenzy. Soon, he drove them both over the edge of something that was incredibly sublime.

"Drink this," she whispered later that night. "It will make you even more of a man and a lover."

"What is it? What are you giving me now?"

"Trust me and drink it!"

"But I *don't* trust you."

Instead of being insulted, Gloria Killion laughed, but it was not a nice sound. "All right, then don't drink it," she said, fingers urging him to a new hardness that he did not think possible.

"Give it to me!" he choked, ashamed of his weakness and trying not to succumb to an overpowering guilt. "But you drink it first."

"You really don't trust me," she whispered, raising up, huge breasts gleaming with drops of perspiration. "All right. I will drink first."

And she did. Oswald watched her throat move as she

swallowed several times and then she looked down at him and giggled. "So now will you drink?"

"Please," he begged, "what is it?"

Her bruised lips twisted into a sneer. "Oswald, does it even matter anymore?"

"I guess it really doesn't."

"So you will stay here with me instead of leaving for Mexico in search of Natalie?"

"I have to go with Marshal Long. I've been deputized." He took the bottle and drank. "I can't let him go alone."

"He isn't going anywhere," Gloria said, dangling one of her breasts, as big and as succulent as a sweet melon, over his lips.

Oswald thought that he should ask what that meant, but he forgot as soon as his mouth found her breast and her body demanded him back inside her. And, as their passion intensified, he forgot to ask what she had meant about Marshal Long.

They slept and when Oswald heard the crow of a rooster announcing the coming of the dawn, he started suddenly and whispered, "What have I done? Natalie!"

His cry momentarily jarred Gloria from sleep and she mumbled something Oswald couldn't understand. All he knew for certain was that he had lost himself to lust and enjoyed this night so much that he knew, if he stayed, he was beyond hope of redemption. So as the woman began to softly snore again and the rooster continued to crow, Oswald used every ounce of what was left of his shattered willpower and tumbled out of bed. He dressed quickly and found his hat, gun and holster, then opened the door.

Zona was standing in the hallway clutching a silk night-gown to her body. She looked past him into the bedroom and, when she saw her older sister, she cried, "What about your beloved Natalie?"

The hallway was dimly lit by lanterns and Oswald re-alized that there were tears running down the girl's cheeks. Her voice carried such searing accusation that he didn't know what to say. There was nothing he could do to redeem himself in her eyes or even in his own.

"What about her?" Zona repeated, her voice a hiss not like that of a cornered cat. "Or what about *me*?"

"I'm sorry."

"Get out of this house! Go to Mexico and die!"

Oswald tried to reach out and touch the girl but her fingernails viciously raked his cheek. He barely felt the physical pain. "Zona, I deserved that. I deserve anything you say or do to me now."

"Go away!"

Oswald glanced back over his shoulder. Gloria was awake now, sitting bare-chested on his bed and wearing nothing but a look of pure triumph. "Zona, I am sorry. Good-bye."

He rushed past her intent on getting his horse from the stable and going to Mexico alone. He didn't deserve to find Natalie or be a deputy, but he would try even if it meant almost certain death.

Tearing his badge from his shirt, Oswald hurled it across the ranch yard at the rooster who danced and then crowed even louder. A few minutes later, he threw himself into the saddle and set the horse running hard for the border. In the blazing light of sunrise and through the shame of his own bitter tears, he could see once beautiful faces now twisted with mockery and disappointment.

Natalie. Zona. Gloria Killion, with her huge luscious breasts and that look of contemptuous triumph.

Oswald began to whip his horse, urging it to run even faster and not at all caring about what happened to him anymore.

Chapter 12

Veronica Killion stood beside her two daughters and watched the dust trail heading south. "What," their mother asked, "happened to make him run away like that?"

Zona whirled on her mother and cried, "Gloria and Oswald went to bed together last night! She seduced him!"

"I did not," Gloria snapped.

"Oh no, then how come you were in *his* bed and not the other way around?"

Gloria hadn't thought about that but managed to blurt, "Because Oswald begged me to come to his room. I thought he was sick . . . or just wanted to talk."

"Liar!" Zona cried.

Gloria's hand shot out and she slapped her younger sister's face, then said, "The trouble with you, Zona, is that you just can't accept the fact that your fallen saint found me more desirable than you or Natalie."

Zona turned on her heel and stormed back into the house, tears streaming down her cheeks.

"She'll get over it in time," their mother said. "But I wish she hadn't caught you in Oswald's bed. Couldn't you at least have lured him into your bedroom so it would have looked better?"

"No."

"Well," Veronica said, "I thought you'd do better than that. At any rate, just leave Zona alone for a few days until she gets over this childish heartbreak. I don't think that we'll ever see young Oswald alive again. He has no idea of what he will face once he crosses into Mexico."

"I say good riddance."

"By the way, how was he in bed?"

Gloria shrugged and then she giggled. "Actually, considering he was a virgin, Oswald was pretty good. I'd say that, if he'd have gone back to Tucson, he'd have impressed the women. And what about Marshal Long?"

"He was *wonderful*. I'll keep him drugged and locked in the bedroom until I've tired of his body."

"But that could be dangerous."

"I don't see how. The drug is so powerful that the man is almost paralyzed except for the part of his anatomy that I need to satisfy myself."

Gloria raised her eyebrows in question. "Maybe you'd let me sample what it is that you've found so much to your liking."

"I think that you've had enough," Veronica said.

"Mother, you're completely selfish!"

"Of course I am. I never denied the fact."

"And what will we do with Marshal Long when you've finally been satisfied? We can't allow the man to escape."

"An overdose," Veronica replied. "I will simply give the marshal an overdose and he'll die in his sleep. Then we can have him removed."

Gloria was satisfied. "All right. But don't take any chances and I would think that even you would have had enough of Marshal Long by tomorrow."

"Maybe," Veronica said. "A man completely under your control is not a power so easy to let go."

"But Marshal Long is dangerous! Don't push your luck, Mother."

"Stop worrying so much. I'll have the marshal in the ground soon enough."

"I hope so. I don't like the idea of you having all the fun."

"Pick one of our cowboys and go hump him in the hay," Veronica said. "Just remember not to bring him into my house. That's always been the rule."

"Yes, Mother."

When her mother turned back to the house, Gloria said, "When Marshal Long is dead, we need to bury him where he can never be found."

"We can use Jesse and Conrad. I trust them with my life."

"You're trusting them with *my* life, too. And the Black Scorpion Ranch as well. If we were caught, the only one left standing would be our weak, foolish Zona."

"I know that," Veronica said a moment before she hurried back to her bed and her drugged federal marshal.

As the sun was dipping into the western horizon, Oswald didn't know when or where the notorious border town of Spur was or even the border itself. He was so tired and hot he really didn't care. After a full day's ride, he was feeling better now, but still wracked with guilt. How could he have allowed himself to be so weak? What would he say to Natalie, even if he found her? Could he admit that he had revered her for years only to allow himself to be taken by another woman last night?

He dismounted then led his buckskin along the lonely road. His poor gelding was suffering from the long day's ride and the heat and badly needed water. Was he in Mexico yet? Oswald was only sure of one thing and that was that he had followed this miserable road south all day. Would there be a sign that said he was in Mexico? Probably not. And as for the town of Spur, maybe he had taken the wrong fork in the road a few miles back. If so, it was too late to retrace his steps. They needed water and then rest and they needed both of them right now.

Heat waves shimmered in the fading light and Oswald's throat was so parched that he could barely swallow. He had heard that it helped to suck on a small stone but he was afraid that the stone would stick to his tongue and he'd maybe swallow it and choke in this miserable dust. This was such a dry and hard country. Where was Spur or even a poor Mexican village? A mud hut or a barn would be a welcoming sight. Oswald had money in his pockets. Maybe there was still hope of redeeming himself and finding his Natalie. And perhaps, someday, he would confess and ask for her forgiveness.

With these thoughts in mind, Oswald Miller began to feel a little better. He would, after all, not be the first man to dishonor himself because of a bad woman. And Gloria Killion *was* a bad woman. Not because of what she had done to his now sinful soul, but because she had done it with such lust and calculated malice.

"I will pray more," Oswald decided. "I have never been a very prayerful or religious man, but I will do better on that front. God will forgive me and so will Natalie . . . if she is yet alive."

And so, with renewed commitment to his quest, Oswald prayed as he continued down the road with the sunset turning the hot Sonoran Desert to molten bronze. It wasn't until long after dark that he saw a small collection of lamps in the distance. There were enough of them that he thought they were either the infamous town of Spur or a very large rancho.

"There will be water and feed for you there," he told the buckskin gelding as he remounted and urged it into a shambling trot.

It took much longer than expected to approach the lights. When they were only just ahead, Oswald reined in the gelding and listened for a few minutes to the sound of guitars playing, laughter and songs spoken in Spanish. But now and then, he also heard whoops and hollers and words in English. Encouraged, Oswald patted the pistol on his lean hip and rode down a dusty street past adobe houses until he came upon a square filled with people dancing and singing to the music.

No one seemed to notice him as he reined the buckskin toward a fountain where it shoved its muzzle deep into the water and drank in great gulps.

"Hey!" a white man yelled in anger. "You can't let a horse drink in the public fountain!"

Oswald yanked hard on the reins attempting to pull the beast's head from the fountain but the gelding was so thirsty he couldn't budge it an inch.

"Get that horse out of there! That is where the people get their water," the man shouted over the sound of the music as he strode forward looking as if he were bent on tearing Oswald from the saddle and killing him on the spot.

"I'm sorry, but where is the horse watering trough?"

"Over there," the man said, pointing to a dim wooden trough near a crowded hitching rail. "If folks see that you are letting a horse drink in their fountain, there will be hell to pay."

Unable to wrench the animal's head around, Oswald dismounted, grabbed the bit and managed to wrestle the buckskin back from the fountain. It didn't want to leave the water, but the man helped him lead the truculent animal over to the horse trough.

"Don't you know anything?" he demanded waving a bottle of tequila in Oswald's face. "Why, there are men here who would kill you for allowing that to happen."

"I didn't know it was wrong," Oswald said. "And anyway, my horse was practically dying from thirst. I'm sorry."

"You are not only sorry, but stupid."

"I have many faults, but I'm not stupid. Ignorant of things down here south of the border. I plead guilty. But never stupid."

"And you talk way too damned much," the man decided.

He was tall, like Oswald, but heavier and wore a full beard. His dusty and wrinkled clothes were what a cowboy would wear, but his Mexican spur rowels were huge and scarred the ground as he walked.

"What's your name?"

"Excuse me for a moment," Oswald said, dunking his face into the horse watering trough to cool his fevered brain. He took several deep swallows and, horse water or not, it tasted wonderful.

Raising up and shaking the water from his hair, he said, "My name is Oswald."

"That's a hell of a poor excuse for a name. I'm going to call you Wally."

"I don't like Wally. What's your name?"

"Henry."

"Henry what?"

"Henry is enough of a handle. Down here you don't give people your last name. It just is nobody's damned business. What's your game, Oswald?"

"What do you mean?"

"What do you do?" the man said with impatience while looking at him as if he were simpleminded. "Steal horses? Guns? Cattle? Or do you deal in women or sheep?"

"None of that."

Henry frowned. "Oswald, you must have something to do or you wouldn't have come down here. I steal horses. It's an honorable pastime and I am good at it. Occasionally, I kill someone for someone who has money."

Oswald's jaw dropped and he stared, trying to figure out if this man was serious. "You kill for money?"

"Honorable trade. Most of the ones I've shot have deserved to die. Hell, we *all* deserve to die. It's just a matter of how soon. Right?"

"I guess." Oswald motioned toward the music and the dancers. Now that he was close, he could see that there were quite a few Americans of the roughest cut imaginable. "What do all these other Americans do?"

"I wouldn't ask if you value your life."

"Is this Spur?"

"It ain't New York City! Want a drink?"

"How far south to the border?"

"I could almost piss on it from here," Henry declared. "Actually, Spur sort of straddles the border. No one cares, though. This main fountain used to be in Mexico but the well went dry there so it was carried a few hundred yards north and now they say it is in the United States of America. Don't matter none to anyone down here. One country is as good as the other."

Henry took a long pull on his bottle, then coughed and spluttered. "Oswald, this is pure Gila monster piss and it'll make you randy as a rooster. Want a pull for two bits?"

Oswald shook his head. "It was drink that brought me to shame and ruin last night. I would prefer to find someplace to board my horse and to lay my bedroll down and sleep."

"Don't you want to have some fun first? This celebration is in honor of some important saint. Better have a tootin' good time while you can because the liquor is almost gone and most of the women weighing less than a full-sized Longhorn cow can't be found."

"There is only one woman that I care to find and I don't expect to see her dancing and drinking in this square."

"Why not? Is she a nun or something?"

"No. But Natalie is very special."

Henry guffawed. Oswald could see that the man was probably no older than himself and was missing several

117

front teeth. He slapped Oswald on the back and crowed, "Now you're talking some sense! All women are special! But just what specialty would you like?"

"The woman I'm looking for was kidnapped many years ago. Her name is Natalie. Miss Natalie Quinn."

"A white woman?"

"That's right."

"Ain't but two in Spur and they're real special all right. Both of 'em is tougher than rawhide and uglier than the butt end of a porcupine."

"My Natalie is beautiful. She'd be about twenty-five with reddish-blonde hair and blue eyes."

"I never heard of a woman like that down in this mean country. Maybe this Natalie went back wherever she came from."

"She couldn't. She was kidnapped when she was a girl. I'm sure that she's somewhere in Mexico and I intend to find her no matter how long it takes."

"Why are you so keen on finding her when there are some women here that will do whatever you want them to do for a dollar? Maybe even less than a dollar. Depends on how hungry or how much they've had to drink. Right now, you could probably get a drunk one for two bits."

"No thanks. Where can I find feed for my horse and a place to sleep tonight?"

Henry frowned. "You got American dollars?"

"A few," Oswald said cautiously because he sure didn't trust this man. "But not many."

"I can find you a place to put up yourself and your horse," Henry said. "Follow me. It ain't far."

Henry let the gelding finish slaking its intense thirst, then he led the weary animal along after Henry. They skirted the plaza and passed down a long line of adobe houses to a little stable where a Mexican boy was waiting. Oswald could see that it was a stable for there were at least a dozen other horses tied under a ramada made of poles and laced cactus stems.

In candlelight, the boy smiled and stuck out his hand. Oswald dipped into his pocket and gave him a coin. The boy bit the coin and, apparently satisfied, nodded his head and led the horse over to a manger then tied it securely. He loosened the buckskin's cinch and Oswald heard the horse groan with satisfaction as it began to eat.

"Tell the kid I'd like him to remove the saddle and put it away."

"Better leave the saddle on the back of the horse or someone will steal it for sure," Henry warned. "Say, that's a pretty nice rifle in your saddle boot."

"It's a Winchester repeater."

"Fetch a good price down here if you decide to sell it."

"It's not for sale."

Oswald decided to leave the buckskin saddled figuring that it might be wise to take Henry's advise. Grabbing his saddlebags and the rifle, he said, "Where can I sleep?"

"There's a hotel just up the street. Cost you fifty cents tonight but you'll have to sleep on the dirt floor."

"If I wanted to sleep on dirt, I could just walk out into the desert."

"Yeah," Henry agreed, "you could do that and maybe find yourself cozying up to a couple of rattlesnakes, scorpions or Gila monsters come morning. But it's your call, Oswald. I don't care where you sleep. Just pay me a dollar for leading you here and giving you the benefit of my expert local knowledge and I'm on my way."

"Isn't there someplace I can sleep in a private room on a real bed?"

"I guess you could go to the mayor's house. He rents out rooms but they're costly."

"Lead me to his house."

"Cost you another dollar."

Oswald paid the man and grumbled, "Stealing horses

119

and killing men for money isn't the only way you earn your daily bread."

"What's that?" Henry asked, turning around and taking another shuddering drink.

"Never mind. Just get me to the mayor's house."

"Follow me. Only thing is, you better not try to get in bed with the mayor's wife or he'll have you skinned alive."

"Believe me," Oswald told the man, "other than Miss Natalie Quinn, I have sworn off all women."

"Shee-it," Henry scoffed. "You're talking like a man riding with only one foot in the stirrups."

Oswald didn't know what that meant and he was so tired he really didn't care.

But Henry had ideas. "Say, how you gonna find this Natalie?"

"I have no idea."

"I could ask around. I know about everyone who knows anything in Spur."

Oswald halted in midstride. "Tell you what, Henry. If you hear of a young woman fitting Natalie's description, I'll pay you . . . five dollars."

"Make it ten."

"All right. Ten dollars for information."

"Information alone ain't going to get you that girl back. You'll need someone who knows how to stay alive and keep you alive as well."

Oswald didn't particularly like or trust Henry, but what the man was saying made a lot of sense. To go off on a search alone not knowing Spanish or the people or the country was simply an invitation to disaster. And, if nothing else, Henry looked tough as nails.

"Can you shoot that six-gun you're wearing?" Oswald asked.

"Hell, yes! And I'm damned good with a knife. Few better. Watch this."

Oswald had noticed that Henry wore a sheathed knife on his left hip. And now, the big man brought it up and, with a flick of his wrist, sent the knife spinning twenty feet to bury its blade in a post no thicker than a man's leg. "What do you think of that?"

"Impressive," Oswald said.

Henry went over and retrieved his knife. He inspected the blade then put it back in its leather sheath. "I've killed three men with knife throws. Killed 'em while they were staring at my gun and wondering if I was going to draw on 'em or not."

"All right," Oswald said, convinced that Henry was a good man to have on his side. "If either one of us hears of Natalie then I'll hire you as my guide and bodyguard."

"Maybe you are smart," Henry said, rubbing his stubbled chin. "All right, let's get to the mayor's house and then I'll start making the rounds of the saloons on both sides of the border. If that girl is anywhere within a hundred miles of Spur, I'll hear about it here. But what if she's married, turned fat or ugly and has a passel of brats?"

Oswald sighed. "I know that's a possibility. But I'd want to see her anyway."

"Why?"

"I don't think you'd understand even if I could explain it."

"Don't matter. Long as I get paid. Say, can you shoot that pistol you're packing?"

"I sure can."

"I'll want to see that if and when we hit the trail."

"Fine."

Several minutes later, they came to the mayor's house. Henry knocked loudly and when the door opened, a heavyset Mexican woman appeared. "Yes?" she said in heavily accented English.

"My friend here, as you can see, is a gentleman and he

don't want to sleep on the floor at the hotels. I told him you might be willing to rent him a room. For a good price, that is."

She inspected Oswald from head to toe and then nodded. "One American dollar a night, senor." Then, she looked at Henry and her eyes narrowed. "But I not let you sleep in my house."

"Fine with me," Henry said, clearly trying not to show that he had been grievously offended. "I got my own bed when I have the need and I sure don't need yours, ma'am."

"Go away then."

Henry turned on his heel and marched off with a stiff back.

"That one is a pig and not to be trusted," the woman said.

"Thanks for the advice but I'd already figured that much out. I sure appreciate you allowing me to . . ."

"You dollar now, please."

"Oswald paid the woman and went inside. She closed, then locked her door and showed him to a spare but clean room. The bed had a real mattress and clean sheets. There was water in a white porcelain pitcher on the nightstand and a clean glass.

"If you need to eat, it will be another dollar."

"I sure could stand to eat."

"You are too skinny."

Oswald could have told the woman that she was too fat but he wisely held that opinion.

"We have already eaten, but you may come to my kitchen when you have taken a bath. I will have my maid bring you hot water."

"Thank you," Oswald said with relief.

"It is nothing. You don't look as if you should be in Spur."

"You don't either, senora."

"*Gracias*. But this is my home. This is my house and my husband is a very important man in this town. He owns two saloons. Very much money he is making. We have a good life in a bad place. *Comprende?*"

"Yes, I do."

With that, the woman of the house left him and went off to tell her maid to get the bathwater hot and to prepare a meal from the evening's leftovers.

Oswald closed his door and expelled a deep breath. He was very tired and he knew that he smelled bad from the long, hot day of travel. But at least he was safe in a good house and he had found someone who was even now asking about Natalie.

Perhaps, he thought, *I will succeed after all and despite my terrible sin with Gloria.* He said a quick prayer of thanks and removed his gunbelt and then his boots. He hoped that his horse and saddle would be safe for the night. Oswald counted his money and it totaled over three hundred dollars. It was a lot of cash to carry and, as he waited for the maid to bring his bath, he decided that he would keep most of it hidden in his boots from now until he found Natalie.

"I wonder how Marshal Long is doing," he said aloud, thinking about how he'd disgraced himself and had, therefore, probably lost any chance of ever being the marshal's sworn deputy. "I sure messed up that opportunity. I wonder if the marshal found my badge in the ranch yard and what he is thinking of me right now. Probably not much."

Discouraged and hoping that he and the marshal from Denver would cross paths down in Mexico, Oswald carried the faint hope that he might yet redeem himself.

Tomorrow would be a new day and on a new day, good things could happen. Maybe, maybe Henry would even tell him that he knew where they could find his dear, lost Natalie Quinn.

Chapter 13

In the morning, Oswald was given a good breakfast and felt ten times the man he had the previous evening. He headed back to the stable and was relieved to find that the boy was still awake and still watching the horses.

"You've done me an important service," he told the lad as he gave him a handful of coins, enough to cause the boy to beam with pleasure. "Do you know where I might find my friend, Henry?"

The boy probably did not understand a lot of Oswald's request but he did know the name and he pointed and s aid, "Cantina. *Mucha cerveza.*"

"Yeah. Which cantina?"

"Red Burro."

"Thanks." The boy looked very sleepy so Oswald added, "I won't be long."

He found the Red Burro and Henry asleep at a back table. Even from a distance the man smelled terrible and looked even worse. Henry was, Oswald decided, bent on self-ruin and dissipation. Still, he knew his way around this lawless country and how to stay alive.

"Henry? Henry!"

The man moaned and when Oswald shook him he finally stirred and opened his bloodshot eyes which failed to focus. "Yeah?"

"It's me. Oswald."

"Who?"

"Oswald Miller. The man you said you'd help for a fee. Did you learn anything about my Natalie?"

Henry's head was resting on his dirty forearm but now he raised it and asked, "I'm really in pain and I need a couple of drinks. Would you buy me a bottle of whiskey?"

"No."

"Please."

"You've had enough for a while. What about Natalie?"

"How about a half bottle?" Henry pleaded. "For gawd's sake, Oswald, at least buy me a couple of lousy beers! I'm dyin'!"

"All right."

Oswald went over to the bartender who looked nearly as dissipated as Henry and as sleepy as the Mexican stable boy. "Two beers."

"Beer ain't gonna do nothing to help him, mister. Better give him a couple of stiff belts of whiskey."

"Fine."

"What are you drinkin'?"

"Nothing."

"You got to drink something," the bartender carped. "I ain't here to admire your looks."

"All right! Three whiskies."

"Might as well take a half bottle," the bartender suggested. "You pay the same price but get more liquor."

"I'm not sure that more liquor is a good idea."

"Think again. You see, Henry is mean when he has a hangover. I was you, I'd take the half bottle and save the money and some grief."

"How much?"

"Three dollars."

"That's outrageous!"

"Henry has killed men who bother him when he's hurtin'. He might kill you too, mister. Three dollars is a bargain when it might save your life."

"Oh, very well! Give me a half bottle," Henry said, slamming the money down on the bar top.

"You don't have to be so sore. I just might have saved your life, you know. Maybe a little thank-you wouldn't hurt."

Oswald shook his head, took the half bottle over to the table and then realized he needed glasses. When the bartender set out a pair, they were so filthy that Oswald only took one for Henry and then he marched back to the table, shook the horse thief and man killer into a state of semi-consciousness and poured him a glass.

Henry eyed the glass, blinked and tried to focus. He next eyed the bottle and grabbed it by the neck. Throwing it upward, he drank like a man dying of thirst and when the bottle was drained, he sighed and then stared at the glass of whiskey.

"Ain't you gonna drink it up? Better not leave that whiskey sittin' there in front of me, Oswald."

"Go ahead."

"Thanks, partner," Henry said with genuine gratitude as he snatched the whiskey glass up and drained it to the last drop. "Ah, sweet salvation! And not a moment too soon."

"Henry, did you find out anything about my Natalie?"

"Who?"

"Natalie! The young woman with the reddish colored hair and blue eyes that was kidnapped years ago. She's the reason I came down here, remember? Last night you promised to ask around about her and fill me in this morning."

"Oh yeah." Henry wiped his sweaty brow. It was warm in the saloon, fetid and airless.

"Why don't we go outside and get some fresh air?"

Oswald suggested. "A little fresh air and maybe a dunk in the horse trough would do you good."

"Sunlight is hard on a man after a week of celebration," Henry muttered, shaking his head back and forth and looking as if he might suddenly vomit. "Still don't feel too damn frisky."

"Maybe I should find someone else to help me find Natalie," Henry said, turning to leave the wreck of a man.

"No, wait! I did hear something about a woman who matches that description."

Henry spun around toward the table. "You did?"

"Sure."

"Where is she?"

"Who?"

"Natalie, gawdammit!"

"Oh, yeah. Well, I think she's down in a little town called Chili."

"I never heard of it."

"Not many have. It's just a Mexican farming village located in a small valley up in the mountains. I've heard that it's a nice place but that the people there are very poor."

"How far?"

"Two, maybe three days' ride to the southwest."

"Then let's go!"

"Hold on now!" Henry grumbled. "We can't just jump on our horses and race south."

"Why not?"

"We need provisions. More ammunition and some grain for our horses. We need some whiskey and . . ."

"No more whiskey. Not until we reach Chili and find Natalie."

"No more whiskey?" Henry said, looking astonished. "Mister, you don't know what you're asking of me."

Oswald reached for his wallet, found ten dollars and laid it down on the poker table. "There," he said with disgust. "I told you I'd pay ten dollars for information. All right. We're square and I don't need your damned help anymore."

Oswald headed outside and was halfway to the stable when Henry overtook him. The larger man grabbed him by the shoulder, spun him around and said, "You won't live to reach Chili without me."

"That's my decision."

Henry was still in bad shape but his hand stabbed downward for his gun. Before he could even clear leather, the barrel of Oswald's Colt rammed into his stomach.

"Don't," Oswald warned.

Henry froze and his bloodshot eyes grew round with surprise then fear. "Say," he choked, forcing a weak laugh, "you're fast!"

"Fast enough, and I generally hit what I aim for," Oswald said. "Now back up, turn around and get lost. You got my ten dollars and I've already bought you a half bottle of whiskey. All for a rumor of Natalie that might not even pan out. We're more than even."

"But . . ."

"Raise your hands, back up, then turn and walk away," Oswald repeated, cocking back the hammer to his pistol. "Henry, I won't ask you again."

"You'd shoot me?"

"If I have to."

"Damn!" Henry muttered, starting to back up. "And here I thought you were a gentleman."

"Get out of here!"

Henry wheeled around unsteadily and weaved his way back down the street. When he was out of sight, Oswald holstered his gun and muttered, "Good riddance."

He paid the Mexican stable boy another coin and mounted his horse. He would ride back to the mayor's house where he would retrieve his Winchester and bedroll, then stop to purchase a few supplies for the trip. It all shouldn't take more than an hour, then he would head south toward a little Mexican village named Chili.

What would he find there? Natalie? And, if so, would she be the wife of some poor peasant farmer?

Oswald steeled himself for that very real possibility. It was also possible that Henry had simply made up the story. Maybe even the name of the farming village. He would find out soon enough. Either way, Oswald figured that he was ready to shake the dust of this miserable town and be on his way deep into Mexico.

At the mayor's house, he was again greeted by the man's wife and when he asked her about Chili, she said that there was, indeed, such a village but that it was so remote and unimportant that she had never known anyone to go there.

"Thank you."

"What do you expect to find in Chili other than poor corn and bean farmers?"

"The only woman that I will ever love."

She looked at him as if he were daft. "In Chili?"

"I hope so."

"Maybe, senor, you have been riding in the sun too long."

"Maybe," he replied, amused because the woman obviously thought he was not of a right mind. "Thank you for your hospitality."

"You are welcome back at this house again," she said quite formally. "Be careful, senor. This is a bad country filled with many bad men. I see you have a fine horse and saddle. And I know you have at least a little money. Those things will attract bandits like honey attracts flies."

"I appreciate your warning."

She watched as he mounted the buckskin and when Oswald tipped his hat to the senora, she shook her head sadly. "I don't think you will find the woman you love in Chili. I don't even think you will find a woman that you can *pay* to love in Chili. The people who live in those little villages are very poor but also very religious. Their Catholic church and their priest is everything, so you had better not insult a woman there or they will send you to hell in a big hurry."

"I never insult women."

Oswald rode south across the border into Mexico which was no different than just north of the border. He saw both Americans and Mexicans working and lounging in the shade of saloons, hotels and liveries. People stared at him as he rode past and no one waved or smiled. Oswald had the impression that they were studying him as if he were an animal about to be slaughtered.

He was glad when he finally struck open country. The land was dry and hot as expected. There were many cactuses and a lot of it was cholla, the black kind with the long and wicked spines. He saw a thin coyote watching him from a rock and a tarantula slowly made its way across the deeply rutted path that could hardly be called a road. The temperature was already approaching one hundred degrees.

At midmorning, Oswald realized that he had no idea whatsoever where Chili was to be found and that he needed to find someone to give him directions. That problem was conveniently solved when he came upon an old man leading an overburdened burro carrying firewood.

"Senor," he said. "*Por favor*. Chili?"

The wood gatherer patted his shrunken belly and grinned.

"No, the village."

The Mexican nodded and smiled his best but said nothing.

"Chili?" Oswald repeated, raising both hands and looking this way and that way.

"Ah, Chili!"

Relieved, Oswald cried, *"Si!"*

The old man raised a hand that protruded from a ragged shirtsleeve. He pointed southeast and said, "Chili."

Oswald tried to find out how far it was and if there was a road that led to Chili, for he did not wish to strike out across this lonely, deadly country with only a single canteen of water. But the old man did not understand and was not overly interested in this poor excuse for conversation. He too was hot and pulled his wide sombrero close over his dark eyes.

Oswald gave the poor man a dollar which elicited a cry of joy. Then, the wood gatherer whacked his sad burro on its rump with a stick and continued on toward Spur.

"Well," Oswald said, removing his hat and wiping his brow as he gazed into the most hostile wilderness imaginable. "I guess I had better head off in the direction that he pointed."

But the going was very slow and difficult. Oswald kept running into immense patches of the wicked cholla. Sometimes, he was forced to ride into deep, dry arroyos. Often, he saw rattlesnakes in the shade and the buckskin grew cantankerous and skittish. Each time they came out of an arroyo, the heat seemed far more intense and, soon, Oswald was hopelessly lost. So lost that he was not even sure which direction was southeast anymore.

"We're lost," he told the buckskin as they stood in the middle of the arroyo hearing only the sound of flies buzzing. "We need to find some shade before both our brains are fried."

He found shade under a stand of barely alive cottonwoods that were hugging a dry streambed. Oswald dismounted and tied the horse in what shade there was available, then loosened the animal's cinch. He collected his rifle and canteen, then crawled a little deeper into the shade and sat down, sweating profusely. He surveyed his surroundings and tried to clamp down on his rising sense of panic.

Overhead he saw a vulture circling against a cloudless sky. Flies buzzed, but nothing else he could see moved. *This is*, he thought, *the most desolate country I have ever beheld*. As the minutes ticked by slowly, Oswald was aware that it would be very easy for a man like himself to end up dead in this situation. Little water, lost and with a horse that was already suffering.

"I can follow my tracks back to the road and get out of this alive," he said, trying to bolster his flagging spirits. "It's clear to me now that I should have waited and sobered up Henry. The man was a degenerate and a drunk, but at least he'd not have led me into this kind of a fix."

Just as Oswald was realizing his mistakes, he heard the striking of hooves on rock and when he jumped up with the rifle in his hands, around the bend in the wide, dry arroyo came Henry.

"Lost, are you?" the horse thief shouted.

"Hell, no!"

"You look lost to me. This arroyo don't lead nowhere but to a hard and thirsty death. I'd say you need a good guide to get you out of this hell."

"How much?"

"Fifty dollars to get you to Chili. More if the girl isn't there and we need to go farther to find her."

Oswald cussed and reached for his wallet because he was in no position to bargain. He had the money and, like it or not, he was going to have to pay the price or suffer the consequences.

Chapter 14

Longarm was not sure how many days or nights had passed since he had been poisoned. Once, he awoke choking and thrashing as someone tried to pour something down his throat that wasn't like anything he'd ever tasted. He'd spat and struggled but his limbs seemed numb and powerless and he'd ended up swallowing several gulps of whatever poison that was being forced upon him.

But now, as he awoke in the darkness, he realized that feeling had returned to his extremities. He was also aware that he was lying naked beside an equally naked Mrs. Veronica Killion. Not wishing to awaken her until he was standing upright with a gun in his fist, Longarm eased off the bed and stood in the faint moonlight. He was shaky and weak, but his fever was gone as were his clothes, boots and gunbelt.

The woman stirred slightly and he froze, heart pounding. Where was Oswald? Dead? Quite possibly. Longarm waited until his vision was focused and then he crept toward the doorway. He opened the door and stood naked and unsure in the hallway for a few moments, trying to decide what to do next. He needed clothes and even more, he needed a weapon in case he chanced upon someone or bumped into something that awakened the household.

Longarm recalled that there were a set of pearl-handled revolvers and a beautifully tooled matching set of holsters and gunbelt displayed in Brendon Killion's impressive office and library. They had, if he remembered correctly, been a gift of General Escobar. There had also been a particularly handsome silver inlaid shotgun. He recalled admiring the double-barreled weapon and realizing that it, like the remarkable set of revolvers, was loaded.

"I don't believe in having a gun that is unloaded," Veronica had told him. "Any more than I'd have a man who was castrated."

The remark had seemed humorous at the time, but not anymore.

Longarm tiptoed into the library and while he was fumbling around trying to find a lamp and matches, he knocked over a tall and heavy hat rack that clashed noisily to the floor.

"Damn," he muttered, jumping toward the door and closing it. He fumbled with the knob and managed to find the lock.

For a moment, he listened, heartbeat loud in his ears. If he awakened the household, then he'd have to find those weapons and prepare to fight his way out of the ranch house. That would be damned near impossible given his weakness and the fact that the bunkhouse was only a short distance from the house and would no doubt be filled with men more than anxious to ventilate his naked carcass.

Longarm hurried over to the window and pushed the heavy curtains open enough to give him some moonlight. Now he spied the prized weapons and snatched the pistols up, one in each hand as he waited for the trouble to start.

But after five minutes of silence, he started to believe that his clumsiness had not awakened the household after all. Longarm took stock of his sorry predicament. He was without clothes and not sure if young Oswald was dead or alive. If the lawyer was still alive, perhaps having also been drugged for the twisted pleasure of the Killion women, then Longarm owed it to his deputy to try and save his life.

"Well, there is only one way to find out," he whispered aloud. "And that's to search the whole damned house."

Longarm knew that, if he did so, he was almost certain to awaken people. But he had no choice. He needed to find out if Oswald was alive and he needed clothes. He sure couldn't try to escape on foot and naked in this hard country because the cactus would tear his feet to shreds before he'd walked a mile.

Longarm felt ridiculous buckling the gunbelt around his waist. Even at the last notch hole, it was still far too loose. Brendon Killion, it seemed, had been a man of considerable girth. Longarm found a set of leather gloves and shoved them between his skin and the gunbelt so that it would not accidentally slip down around his ankles at a critical moment. He also decided to take a fine Stetson, which proved to be his size.

Wearing only a hat and a gunbelt, I must look like a wild and crazy bastard, he thought as he levered a round into the Winchester and started for the door.

He unlocked it slowly and opened it a crack. All was darkness in the hallway and Longarm could not hear a sound. *So far, so good.* He eased out into the hallway bent at a crouch turning one way, then the other, expecting someone to burst out of a bedroom firing. But still not a sound except faint snoring emanating from several bedrooms.

Longarm tried to remember where Oswald had been sleeping and he decided that it had been a room just down the almost pitch-black hallway to the right. He started in that direction, free hand sliding along the wall until he accidentally knocked a large picture loose. Like the hat rack, it struck the floor with a loud bang and Longarm again froze, certain that someone must surely have been awakened by the sound.

And he was right. He saw a thin bead of light materialize at the bottom of a door. Longarm stepped up to the door and, when it eased open, he flattened against the wall.

What happened next was so sudden that he had no time to think but only to react. A form jumped into the hallway and opened fire with a pistol. Longarm saw its muzzle flash but the one pulling the trigger was shooting blind.

Longarm ducked low and squeezed off a rifle shot. In the closed hallway, it sounded like a cannon and the slug knocked the man backward. Only now the bedroom door swung open and Longarm could see that it wasn't a man . . . it was Gloria Killion. She was twitching and thrashing in the hallway and Longarm knew that she was in her death throes.

He knelt by her side and hissed, "Where is Oswald? Where is my deputy?"

She made a bubbly sound and then uttered a curse before shuddering her way into a well deserved hell.

Longarm could hear shouting from the bedrooms and when someone else was foolish enough to emerge into the death and confusion, they were greeted the same way as Gloria and with the same fatal results.

"Oswald!" Longarm yelled, bursting into the room where he thought his friend from Tucson had been assigned. "Oswald!"

The bed was a tangled mess, but it was empty. Longarm heard the pounding of feet in the hallway and then screams of both men and women.

It was time to go.

He used the butt of Killion's prized rifle to smash his way through the window. Glass cut him as he made his escape into a large courtyard graced by a pond, large shade trees and many wooden tables, chairs and benches. Longarm didn't care. Running for his life, he scaled a low wall and lit out for the stable. If he could reach a horse, there was yet a chance of escape given the cover of darkness. But now, moonlight was his worst enemy.

He heard shots from the house and then the sound of bullets striking the ground and the buildings toward which he ran. A light flickered on in the bunkhouse and its door burst open just as Longarm cleared the last few feet of open ground and dove into the stable. Shaky and covered with sweat that now caked his body in mud, he jumped up and ran headlong into someone who must have slept nights in the barn.

They both went down and Longarm lost his grip on the rifle. The man swore and got up first. He kicked blindly, hoping to strike flesh, but missing, he fell again. Longarm drew one of the pistols and it took him three swings before he cracked his opponent's skull with a sickening and familiar crunch.

Jumping up, Longarm retrieved the Winchester, ran into a post, tripped over a wheelbarrow and finally reached the large back door of the barn. Moonlight again and now horses. Lots of horses. They were nervous and it was all he could do to stay calm enough to say, "Easy. Easy horses. It's all right."

Longarm knew it wasn't a matter of *what* he said but instead how he spoke that counted. The horses were in a huge round corral and there were probably at least twenty. Maybe thirty. They were milling around and had probably been selected as the mounts to be used for this coming day's ranch work.

Longarm saw saddles, blankets and bridles resting on the top rails and he leaned his rifle against the lower rail, grabbed a bridle and moved toward the nearest horse.

"Easy now," he said, aware that he had very little time

before his location was guessed by those who would try to kill him. "Easy."

The horse was tall and dark. Probably a black, but possibly a bay. It whirled and ran to join its friends, still circling, nostrils extended and snorting.

"Easy," Longarm repeated over and over as he cut into the flow of horseflesh and managed to get his arms around one of their necks. He planted his bare heels in the dirt to brake the horse but it stepped on him and he howled with pain. The horse broke free and Longarm spilled to the dirt in real danger of being trampled to death.

He got up and had no choice but to drop the pretense of being calm. Racing into the milling mass of horses, he jumped onto the back of one animal, leaned forward and grabbed its ear, twisting hard.

The pain brought the horse to an abrupt standstill almost catapulting Longarm over its head. But he clung to the beast like a mountain lion and when he finally got it under control, he jumped down and managed to get the long leather reins around its neck. After that, things got easier. Longarm bitted the horse, also tall and dark, then led it over to the nearest saddle and blanket.

Minutes later, after cinching the saddle down hard, he grabbed the Winchester and strode toward the gate. He only needed another couple of minutes to be free and running for cover.

"There he is!" someone bellowed. "He's in the corral trying to get away!"

Longarm jumped for the gate. It was a large pole gate fixed to the fence with a single tied rope. If Longarm had been carrying a knife, the fastest thing to do would have been to cut the rope. Instead, he used a few precious seconds to untie the knot, push the gate open and then mount his skitterish horse.

A volley of shots filled the night and a horse was struck. It screamed in pain and terror and crashed through

140

the opening. It was like the bursting of a dam only, instead of water, it was fear-driven horses bursting out of the corral in their bid for freedom.

"Hold your fire! You're killin' our horses!" someone cried. "Hold your fire until you see the son of a bitch!"

Longarm had no intention of allowing them to "see the son of a bitch" as he mounted and then drummed his bare heels into his mount's ribs. He was part of a river of rolling thunder as it poured through the half-opened gate, splintering it to pieces.

He stayed as low as he could on the back of the horse and the animal he rode almost lost its footing as it skidded in a sharp turn in the face of the armed line of cowboys. Despite someone's warning, several more shots were fired and another horse went down kicking. Longarm found his stirrups and used the trophy rifle to smack his horse across the rump and send it flying out of the Black Scorpion Ranch yard into the terrible desert.

Horses were still running in a bunch but some had began to peel away and take their own paths in various directions. This was perfect, Longarm thought, because it would confuse the pursuit and force the cowboys to split up into small numbers and follow every trail.

There were about a half dozen horses still in his bunch when they topped a ridge. Aware that he had no water for himself or his horse, and that the footing was treacherous and there was a very real danger of his horse breaking a leg or blundering into cholla, Longarm drew his mount up hard and let the other animals run blindly on into the night.

He looked back at the house and saw that it was ablaze with lights. He knew that the cowboys would be insane with frustration in their desire to find mounts and take up the chase. He also knew that Gloria Killion was dead and that maybe the other person whom he'd shot in the hallway was her mother. At least, he hoped it was the same woman who had used him as her sex slave for how long he could not guess.

But what if he had actually shot Oswald by mistake? Everything had happened so quickly there had not been time to identify his second victim.

Or perhaps it had been the youngest of the three Killion women, Zona.

Longarm sure hoped not. Zona was the only one of those Killion women that seemed even halfway normal and decent.

Chapter 15

Longarm cut across the desert and just about when the sun was peeking over the eastern horizon, he spotted a freight wagon moving south along a dirt road. The high-sided wagon was huge and pulled by six stout mules. Longarm could see two men, one driving and the other was obviously an armed guard.

The wagon was about a mile to the west and, after several minutes of deliberation, Longarm decided that he had no choice but to intercept the wagon and plead his case. He was quite sure that, if he stayed out in the morning sun, his pale skin would soon be blistered red. Still, when the two freighters saw him riding up naked, they might decide to just shoot and put him out of his misery.

"Hello there!" Longarm called, wondering what their reaction would be when they saw him riding naked. "Could you hold up a minute? I need some help."

Longarm didn't like asking anyone for help and when the two men on the freight wagon saw him galloping toward them, their jaws dropped and they stared. Then, the one with the rifle pointed it directly at Longarm who yelled, "Don't shoot!"

The rifleman held his fire and when Longarm got within

perhaps fifty yards, he bellowed, "That's close enough. What the hell are you doin' out here without no clothes!"

"Long story. Do you have any extras?"

The two men exchanged glances and then the driver said, "We ain't got no extra clothes. We're carryin' supplies to Spur from Tucson."

"How about blankets?" Longarm asked hopefully.

"Got a few of 'em but . . ."

"I'm broke," Longarm grudgingly admitted. "But I ought to be able to raise some cash when I sell my outfit."

"You won't live to sell anything if you ride into Spur like that," the guard shouted. "You'd be taken for a crazy man and shot outta the damned saddle."

"I'll pay you when I get some money in Spur. All I want is to tie my horse to the back of your wagon and climb inside. Once I'm in town, I can figure out some way to get dressed again."

"Did the Apache steal your duds?" the driver asked, scratching his head in bewilderment.

Longarm could immediately see that the pair would accept this reasoning and probably no other. "Yep, it was the Apache."

"Well I'll be jiggered!" the guard said, lowering his gun. "They usually steal your scalp instead of your clothes."

"Well, as you can see, I've still got my scalp. So how about a little help?"

The driver nodded, but his mind was still fixed on the Indians. "How many Apache jumped you?"

"There were a bunch."

"And you musta been sleepin' in the naked when they did it and you just grabbed your rifle and gunbelt and lit out for your life. That it?"

"You guessed it right," Longarm replied. "I feel like a complete fool but I figure I am lucky to have saved my hide from those murderin' devils."

"You *are* damned lucky! How come they didn't run you down and finish you off?"

"They were on foot."

"You reckon they're still chasin' you?"

"I don't know," Longarm said, "but I don't like the idea of us sitting here talking about it while they might be getting closer. Hell, they could even be putting us in their rifle sights this very minute!"

The guard's eyes widened and he swiveled one way and then the other looking for ambushing Indians. "Well, mister," he said when he could find no Apache, "we need to get a'movin'!"

"Can I tie my horse in the back and ride inside your wagon until we reach Spur?"

"I guess. If the Apache attack us, we'll need every gun we can use to fight them off. So tie up and let's roll!"

Longarm could not have been a more willing passenger. He drummed his heels into the flanks of his horse and it took him only a couple of minutes to tie the animal to the back of the freight wagon and then to scramble inside.

"I sure appreciate this," he said, settling down on a wooden crate and trying not to get a splinter in his behind.

"There's a couple Indian blankets in that canvas sack. I guess Milt Weber, who has ordered 'em will understand if you use one of them and don't get it too sweaty."

"I'll try not to," Longarm assured the man.

"You could also use a hat to keep the sun off your head," the driver said. "I know that Milt ordered a few Stetsons. Got to be in one of those boxes. Find one and put it on before the sun starts to fry whatever brains you have left."

"Thanks."

"Let's roll!" the guard bellowed, clearly nervous about the Apache that still might be following Longarm.

"How far to Spur?"

"We'll be there by high noon," the guard said, obviously too embarrassed to turn around and address Longarm directly. "If we don't get ambushed and scalped first."

Spur was about what Longarm had expected. He was fortunate in that the supply wagon entered an alley and pulled up behind the general store to unload. Longarm, wrapped in a blanket like a Navajo, jumped down from the back of the wagon and had to suffer the same stares from Weber and two of his employees that he'd gotten from the driver and guard.

After quickly explaining his circumstances, he asked, "I'll need the horse, saddle and some weapons. But I don't need any as fancy as these matched revolvers or the Winchester. How about giving me some clothes and a used handgun and rifle in trade?"

Milt Weber was an older man. Tough looking with shrewd eyes and a sharp mind. "I'd say that you are in no bargaining position."

"You're right about that," Longarm admitted. "But I can probably find someone else to trade off these weapons for clothes."

"Come into my office and we can talk in private," the man said. "Boys, gets these goods unloaded and quit standing around. There's always work to do or you can start looking for a new job."

The men started unloading and Longarm followed Weber through the back part of his building which was for storage. They entered a small but efficient office and Weber closed the door so they could talk in private.

"So, my driver said that you were attacked by Apache and they stole your clothes."

"That's right."

"I don't think so."

"What do you mean?"

Weber reached into his office desk, drew a derringer from the top drawer and leveled it at Longarm. "Because

146

those revolvers and that rifle belonged to my friend, Brendon Killion. So the question is, why are you lying and how did you steal them from Mrs. Killion?"

Longarm hesitated, studying the man. He had no doubt that, in a town as lawless as Spur, Weber could shoot him dead and claim he'd had to do so in self-defense. There'd be no inquiry, no questions asked and Longarm would be buried in an unmarked grave probably without even the benefit of a crude wooden casket. Billy Vail would never be able to track him to his grave and his sorry fate would remain forever unknown.

"I'm waiting, but you're about to run out of time," the man said.

"All right," Lognarm told him. "My name is Custis Long and I'm a Deputy United States marshal sent from Denver to find out what really happened to Marshal Scotty Atkinson and three Arizona Rangers."

Weber's expression didn't change. "Go on."

"That's it."

"No, it's not. You haven't said how you got Brendon's prized weapons. He brought them in here to show them off to me."

"I was a guest at the Black Scorpion Ranch. Mrs. Killion gave the weapons to me."

"Liar!" Weber hissed as he cocked the deadly little pistol. "Veronica hates all lawmen."

"Well," Longarm said, realizing he was about to be shot dead, "she had better change her attitude because, if you kill me, there will be federal officers swarming all over her ranch and this town. Too many of us have died already."

"No one would ever find out what happened to you in this office," Weber said, his finger tightening on the trigger.

Longarm wasn't going to sit still and take a bullet. Not without a fight, he wasn't. Trouble was, he stood no chance whatsoever of avoiding being shot dead, so he made one last attempt to save his life with reasoning.

"Listen," he told the store owner. "You look like an intelligent man and you've obviously done well here. But if you kill me, you'll lose everything and you will wind up walking the gallows. I was seen by a lot of people today and all of them are going to remember me because I was wearing nothing but a hat and a blanket. People are going to remember that I was in your supply wagon and delivered to your loading dock. So why risk losing everything unless you've done something that is going to get you hanged."

"Like what?"

"Like having a part in the killing of either my friend, Scotty Atkinson, or those Arizona Rangers."

"I had nothing to do with them! Nothing at all!" the man spluttered in anger. "I'm a businessman . . . not a revolutionary."

"Prove it," Longarm challenged. "Put the gun away and that will tell me more than words that you can be trusted. I need someone in Spur that I can trust. Maybe you're the man."

"Why should I help you?"

"Because, if you don't kill me, then you've no choice. You admitted that you were good friends with Brendon Killion."

"I didn't say that we were *good* friends. We probably weren't even friends. We drank a lot of whiskey together and I used to skin him pretty good at cards. In fact, the money I won from Brendon at the table helped me buy this business. I never let him forget that and it worked hard at his craw."

"You were friends."

"We were both businessmen," Weber insisted. "But his business and my business were entirely separate. He was a rancher and I'm a store owner. He liked to play politics along this border and hobnob with Mexican revolutionaries. I never cared for that sort of thing. I told him it would be his ruin, but he wanted power and he liked to be around what he thought were powerful people. He used to say that it gave him a bigger boost than whiskey."

Longarm nodded toward a cuspidor. "I could use a cigar right now and a shot of good whiskey."

"Maybe I'll shoot you instead," Weber suggested, the derringer still cocked and aimed at Longarm's chest.

"Maybe, but I doubt it. Either way, make your move."

Weber turned the pistol aside and replaced it in his drawer. "I've killed men who robbed or cheated me, but I've never shot a man in cold blood and I'm too old to start doing it now. But I ain't sure what to believe of your story. You've lied some to me and now you want me to believe that you're telling the truth."

"Sometimes," Longarm said, "a man has to take things on faith. Why would I lie about being a federal marshal here in a town like Spur where that admission is most likely to get me shot?"

"Good point."

"So what kind of cigar do we smoke and where's the whiskey? And while we're at it, how about a good set of clothes?"

"You're a demanding bastard, ain't ya?"

"How would you like to be wearing this damned wool blanket in this heat?"

Weber's face suddenly creased into a smile and he laughed. "All right. First the whiskey and cigar, then some clothes."

"Good clothes," Longarm said. "Your best. I don't want any shabby work duds . . . not in exchange for these prized weapons."

"Which you must have stole from Mrs. Killion."

"She drugged me and planned my death," Longarm said, deciding not to mention the rest of the sordid story or anything about Oswald Miller, who was probably dead but might still be alive.

"So what happened to her?" Weber said, taking a cigar and stuffing it in his mouth, then offering one to Longarm. "I know Veronica would never have let you leave her ranch alive."

"She had no choice."

"Is she . . . still alive?"

Longarm snatched a match from the desk, lit his cigar and squinted through the smoke. "Good cigar."

"Thanks. Now answer my question, Marshal Long."

"Mrs. Veronica Killion is most certainly dead," Longarm answered. "I had no choice but to kill her an instant before she would have killed me."

"That's good *and* bad news."

"What do you mean?"

"The good news is that if Veronica is really dead, then this town will celebrate as if it were the Fourth of July. She was the power behind the scenes. Brendon didn't like to hear that, but it was his wife who was a threat to anyone she suddenly took a dislike to. She wanted this store and, when I refused to sell, she threatened to have me eliminated."

"But didn't."

"Brendon got word of it and he let Veronica know that I was to be left alone. Otherwise . . ."

Weber didn't need to finish. Longarm understood. He watched as the store owner found two clean glasses and a bottle. Longarm raised his glass in salute and said, "So you're going to keep quiet about who I am and what happened at the Black Scorpion Ranch?"

"I don't need to tell anyone. If you did kill Mrs. Killion, the whole town will know it soon enough."

"You said the death of Veronica Killion was good news but there was also bad. What's the bad part?"

Weber didn't hesitate. "The bad part is that Gloria Killion will be the next in line to run the Black Scorpion Ranch and control what people do and say in this part of the country. And, for my money, she's every bit as crazy and as much of a she-devil as her mother. There's no telling what she will do next."

"In that case, I have something else I might as well tell you," Longarm said.

"I'm hanging on your every word, Marshal."

"The news is that there is no downside to this because I'm pretty sure that I also shot Gloria Killion to death in that dark hallway."

"Holy shit!" Weber breathed. "Are you serious?"

"Why would I not be?"

"If that's true," Weber mused aloud. "If that's true, then the last Killion standing would be Zona."

"I might have killed her," Longarm admitted. "it was dark and it was fast. But I think it was Gloria that came out of that bedroom with a gun so that I had to shoot."

"I sure hope so!" Weber said fervently. "Zona was the only one in that entire family that had a conscience. She is a good person."

"Good meaning weak, meaning that she'll be easy to deal with and perhaps even take advantage of?"

Weber smiled. "I said that Zona was a good person and not crazy like the rest of that bunch. I didn't say that she was weak. To the contrary, she's the only one that had any interest in making an *honest* dollar. I've known her for years and she used to come in here with her mother and sister to buy things. Zona was the only one that would ask normal questions and show any interest in sound business practices."

"Well," Longarm said, "let's hope that she's the only one left standing."

"We'll find out soon enough."

"So what about the death of Marshal Scott Atkinson and the Arizona Rangers?"

"They were shot to death by the Killion men."

"I've heard that before."

"Then believe it, and go back to Denver where you came from before someone else finds out that you're a federal marshal."

"I can't do that," Longarm replied.

"Why not? I told you the truth."

"Which I believe," Longarm said truthfully as he thought about Oswald Miller and a girl named Natalie Quinn who had been kidnapped long ago. "But I have a few other loose ends to tie up first."

"Ends you aren't willing to discuss?"

Longarm took another gulp of whiskey. He studied the man and decided that he really needed someone locally that he could trust. So why not tell Milt Weber about Oswald and the lost love he had hoped to find?

"A long time back," Longarm began, "there was a girl named Natalie Quinn. Her parents were killed and . . ."

"I knew the Quinns."

"You did?"

"Sure. Good people. And I knew their daughter."

"She was taken down into Mexico. I mean to find her."

"Forget about that."

"Why?"

"Because she's either dead or she's married and has a passel of brats."

"I have to find out."

Weber drained his glass. "Why?"

"Because I had a friend who cared deeply about her."

"That doesn't make sense."

"I know, but that's the way of it."

"So you're going to cross the border and look for Natalie?"

"That's my intention."

Weber shook his head. "You come in here wearing nothing but one of my Indian trade blankets. You look

152

like a crazy man and you immediately start telling me lies."

"Sorry about that, but I had my reasons."

"And now you want me to believe you are a federal officer and that you're going after a girl that no one has seen or heard of for years. And you won't tell me why?"

"I guess it all sounds pretty lame," Longarm admitted. "But that's the way of it."

"It's far too crazy not to believe," the man finally said. "All right, Marshal Long . . . if you are Marshal Long . . . I'll outfit you in exchange for those handsome pistols and the special rifle."

"I just need a good pistol and working rifle in addition to new clothes."

"You need more than that. You need a pack mule and lots of other things. Actually, you need an army escort."

"We both know that isn't going to happen."

"Yeah," Weber said, "and that being the case, I'd say you need a priest and a whole lot of luck if you're planning to come back here alive with Natalie Quinn."

Longarm finished his whiskey. "My luck has been running mostly cold lately. Perhaps it is time that changed. Either way, I'm going to Mexico and I'll either find the girl dead or alive. If she's alive, then she can decide if she wants to come back to the United States."

"You've no authority in Mexico."

"I know that."

"The only law down there is the gun. And, if that twisted sadist General Miguel Hernandez Escobar or one of his men get their meat hooks into you, then you'll wish you were never born. And we haven't even mentioned the Apache who would love to roast you alive over their campfire."

"I've heard of all the dangers, but that doesn't change what I have to do. Just trade me some good, straight-shooting weapons."

"I will."

"Then we're done talking."

"Would the feds really have come down here and dug up what happened to you if I'd decided to put an end to your life?"

"You bet they would have."

Weber nodded his head. "They must value you very much, Marshal Long."

"I'd like to think so."

"In that case, I hope they have your replacement because once you ride down deep into Mexico, you are history."

Longarm unbuckled the gunbelt around his hips. "Show me your best clothes and boots," he said. "And I wouldn't mind taking a bath before I head south."

The man laughed. "Why waste the water?"

Longarm didn't really like this man, but he had decided to trust him. Maybe that was why he didn't haul off and knock the smirk and his teeth down Milton Weber's throat.

Chapter 16

Oswald's throat was sandpaper and his eyes were swollen and bloodshot from the blowing dust and terrible dry heat. His horse was suffering as well and he thought he had never seen such bad country as there was in this part of northern Mexico.

"I don't see how anyone could survive, much less farm around here," he croaked, his voice strange sounding even to himself.

Henry pointed ahead. "See those blue mountains just up ahead of us?"

"Yeah."

"How far away do you think they are?"

Oswald was not in the mood for guessing games. "I don't know. Five miles?"

"More like twenty. And just beyond them is a river that runs all the year around and a valley that's green with corn and filled with simple, hard-working peasants."

"Is that the village called Chili?"

"Yep."

Oswald drove his heels into his horse's flanks but, instead of breaking into a gallop or even a trot, the gelding just groaned and kept walking. "Damn horse!"

"Would you run in this heat?" Henry asked as he craned his head up toward the sun. "We need to find some shade and wait out the worst of the heat. We keep riding in this sun, we might not make it to Chili."

Oswald knew the advice was sound, but he'd waited too many years to stop now. "If you want to hunt shade and wait, go ahead. But I'm not waiting anymore. I'm going ahead to see Natalie."

"You're a fool," Henry said dispassionately. "We might kill our horses and then end up on foot. And, if that happened, our chances of reaching the village aren't worth squat."

"I'm not stopping."

"A damn fool! All right, we'll push on and take our chances, but it's a mistake." Henry clamped his cracked lips together and kept riding beside the lawyer.

Two hours of misery passed and the mountains seemed not one bit closer. Still, Oswald knew that they had to be. If his played-out horse was walking even at the rate of three miles an hour, then they'd covered six of the twenty miles and the Mexican village where Natalie might be found was almost within their grasp. Just fourteen more miles. No more than five hours at this brain-baking walk.

Henry leaned out of his saddle and unsuccessfully tried to work up a spit. He hawked and hawked but nothing happened. Next, he reached for his canteen and uncapped it. He sloshed what water remained around for a moment and then decided to recap the canteen and hold on just a little longer. The thought of having a dry canteen in this heat and country was something that his mind would not permit.

"If I had any water left in my canteen, I'd drink it up right now," Oswald said in a raspy voice. "But I drank my canteen empty this morning."

"I know you did, you damn fool."

"Quit calling me that!" Oswald shouted. "Or by gawd I might just . . ."

"Just what?" Henry challenged. "Shoot me? My oh my. Our civilized man of the law is about ready to commit murder. How does it feel to walk on the wild side?"

"Shut up."

"Well," Henry said, "I know how it feels to be so mad, so filled with rage that you want to kill someone. The only difference between you and me, lawyer, is that I just go ahead and act on the impulse. I do what I please while you stew inside."

"It's the difference between a civilized being and a barbarian," Oswald informed him.

"You're calling me a barbarian?"

"I'm saying that civilized people live by laws, not by their basest natures."

Henry smiled and paid the price as his lips split in a new place. "Goodness gracious!" he declared in a mocking tone of voice. "You throw out big words like a gambler throws his cards, but they still all sound like horseshit. Pure, plain old ordinary horseshit!"

Oswald heard the man's brittle chuckle and he chose to ignore it. He focused on the blue mountains up ahead and closed his eyes for a moment, trying to visualize the river and the green fields that he would soon be enjoying. And Natalie. Maybe she would be standing in a tall cornfield with a hoe in her hand or perhaps sitting in the shade making tortillas.

Or, he thought with a painful stab to his heart, *maybe Natalie will be holding a baby to her breast and trying to appease several more children and a lazy, demanding husband.* Oswald didn't like that picture so he opened his eyes and that's when he saw the dozen or so horsemen galloping toward him.

"Henry! We've got company!"

"I know. Just saw 'em myself."

"What shall we do?"

"Nothing to do but to find a place to make our stand. Our horses couldn't run a lick. I can tell by the way that bunch is moving that their mounts are in far better shape than ours."

"Apache?"

"Nope. Mexicans."

Relief flooded through Oswald. "I sure am glad to hear that!"

"I'm not," Henry said, his eyes squinted and his expression hard as he drew his rifle from his saddle boot. "They look like they're on patrol. Unless I miss my guess, this bunch is either the Mexican army or General Escobar's boys. Either way, they're trouble."

"Why?"

"Because they don't make any money and they'll want to steal everything we own. And you can bet that they won't want any gringos as witnesses."

Without another word, Henry reined his horse hard to the right and forced it into a shambling trot toward a cluster of rocks and cactus. It was, Oswald saw, the only good cover for miles. Oswald's heels drummed against the flanks of his horse and the animal wearily responded, probably not wanting to lose the company of Henry's horse.

By the time they reached the cover and dismounted, the Mexicans were already firing. Oswald raised his rifle but he couldn't see because of the sweat stinging his eyes.

"Hold your fire!" Henry ordered. "They're out of range and just seeing how we'll behave under fire. Let's wait 'em out a little longer."

Oswald glanced up at the cloudless, washed-out sky. It was so hot that he felt dizzy. "Henry," he whispered, "I'm in no condition to wait anyone out. Neither are you and neither are our horses. We're out of water and we can't win a waiting game."

"You're right. But neither can we outrun 'em or out-fight 'em."

"So what's left?"

"Surrender and hope for the best."

Oswald shook his head. "But you just said they'd kill us for sure."

"Not if we refuse to give up our guns."

"You mean . . ."

"I mean we give them our horses, saddles and hope that is enough. They don't want to die any more than we do."

"But without horses you said we couldn't make it to Chili!"

"Dammit, Oswald, a man can change his mind, can't he? Maybe I was wrong. Maybe we bargain for a little water as well as our weapons and our lives."

Oswald didn't know what to say as he watched the Mexicans dismount and lead their horses into an arroyo then again open fire with their rifles. They weren't very good shots but they were sure giving it a real show and bullets filled the air thicker than flies at a picnic.

"My snot rag is real dirty. How about yours?" Henry asked.

"Huh?"

"Your handkerchief! We'll wave a white flag which will tell them we want to talk."

"Oh. Right." Oswald found his handkerchief which was pretty filthy but no doubt cleaner than Henry's.

"Find a damn stick and start waving the thing."

Henry kept his head down as the Mexicans began to get their range and the bullets started whanging off the nearby rocks.

"Hurry up!" Henry ordered.

Oswald found a stick and impaled his handkerchief. Keeping his head down low, he began to wave the thing back and forth as the bullets kept creeping closer.

"Hold your fire!" Henry yelled at the Mexicans, then hissed to Oswald. "Let's hope at least one of them speaks some English."

"Come out with your hands empty and up!"

"No dice!" Henry yelled back. "We need water!"

"You get nothing but death if you do not obey my orders!"

"Are you ridin' for General Escobar?"

"*Si!* Who are you?"

"We are looking for a young woman!"

Both Oswald and Henry heard a burst of ragged laughter from the ranks of the revolutionaries. It made them realize that the answer had, indeed, sounded ridiculous.

"We are *all* looking for a young woman. But you are also looking for death, gringo! You do not belong in Mexico. You are invaders. There is no escape and you are in no position to make demands for water or anything else. Now do as I order or we will kill you!"

"If you try, many of you will die," Henry warned. "You might be one of them. Let's talk a trade."

There was a long pause and then, " "I am listening."

"We need to reach the village of Chili."

"Is that where your young woman is waiting?"

"Yes."

"Stupid gringo. You could have found one in Spur or any one of the border towns."

"Maybe that is true, but this one is *very* special," Henry shouted back over enemy hoots and laughter.

"I don't care what she is," the Mexican finally said. "I myself have been to Chili and their women are ugly and too thin from hard work. Throw your guns out now. It is too hot to argue."

"We'll give you our horses but, in exchange, we want two full canteens of water. We have no money."

"I want everything you have, senor!"

"Then you're going to have to die getting it!" Henry

cried, jumping up with his rifle, taking a quick aim and firing.

Oswald was shocked when he heard a scream. "Now you've gone and done it. So much for negotiations."

"I may have only wounded him," Henry said. "I just needed them to feel some pain before they do anything hasty."

Oswald took a deep breath. He heard a sound in his ears like bacon frying and prayed it wasn't his brains. "I sure hope they decide not to try and kill us."

"Me, too."

"Senor!"

"Yeah?" Henry yelled.

"You have wounded one of my best men."

"I could have killed him, but I wanted to show that I am a reasonable man. A man of mercy."

"Ha!"

"How about throwing out two canteens in trade for our horses? No one has to die. Take your wounded man back to wherever you came from or to a doctor before he bleeds to death."

There was another long silence and then, "All right, senor. I agree. Two canteens for two horses."

"Good," Henry shouted.

"Real good," Oswald whispered with a sigh of relief.

"Send out the horses, gringo."

"First throw out the canteens and I'll be able to tell if they have water in them or not."

"How can you do that?" Oswald asked.

"I can't, but it sounded good. Keep a sharp eye in case they try anything tricky."

"Like what?"

"Like sneaking up behind us."

"Oh."

Two leather bound canteens were thrown out into the open. They didn't bounce off the hard ground and so Oswald thought they might actually contain water.

"Now turn loose your horses!"

Henry extracted an extra revolver and a box of cartridges from his saddlebags. Oswald removed his money. They tied their reins to their saddle horns and spanked their geldings out of the rocks. The animals could hear and smell the Mexicans' mounts and moved forward with more enthusiasm than they'd shown since leaving Spur.

"All right," Henry yelled. "Now ride on and leave us in peace."

The Mexican negotiator laughed and it had an unpleasant sound.

The Mexican's laughter was high and taunting. "We will go because I say we will go. And maybe me and my men will ride to Chili and see your beautiful young woman. If she is there, I will mount her first and then let my soldiers of the revolution all take their turns."

"Bastard!" Henry yelled.

The Mexicans howled with laughter. But, to Oswald's surprise, they did come out of the arroyo and help the wounded man into the saddle before they rode away.

"You think they'll leave us alone?" Oswald asked.

"I have no idea, but I wouldn't bet on it," Henry said, his face grim and troubled. "They know we are well armed but I'll bet they think we also have plenty of American dollars."

"Then what have we gained?" Oswald asked with bitterness.

"A bit of time. And there's something else we have to worry about."

"What's that?"

"Did you count how many came and how many rode away just now?"

"No."

"Neither did I. Some might still be hiding in the arroyo waiting for us to come out for the canteens."

Oswald swore. "So what do we do now?"

"The only thing we can do. We'll stay in the rocks until darkness and then sneak out and grab those two canteens. Then, we'll strike out for Chili. Once in the village, maybe we can find your Natalie and figure out how to get back to our side of the border."

"Good plan," Oswald mumbled, closing his eyes and hearing the bacon start to sizzle again on his brain pan.

He must have fallen asleep because the sun was down and darkness was finally covering the tortured land when Henry nudged him into wakefulness.

"It's time to get those canteens. Keep a sharp eye out and your finger on the trigger. They might have left one or two of their best marksmen behind to nail us when we come out into the open."

"How could they see us?"

"There is still enough of a moon to give them shooting range. The ground is white and we'll be dark, moving shadows. I could hit a man from thirty or forty yards with my rifle."

"Not a comforting thought," Oswald decided out loud. "Maybe we should just forget the canteens and slip off in another direction."

"Yeah, maybe. But we might not make it to the village on foot without water."

Oswald knew his horse thieving friend was right. How many more miles to the mountains and then to Chili? He could see their dark spine in the distance and wasn't at all sure he could reach them, given his intense thirst and suffering.

Henry drew his pistol and pushed himself up into a crouch. He took several deep breaths, then hissed, "Let's go!"

Oswald followed the man with both his heart and his head pounding wildly. They were in a terrible fix and he wasn't a bit sure they would survive the night even if the revolutionaries kept their end of the bargain.

"Almost there," Henry grunted. "Gawd, I hope those canteens are filled with water!"

They were both too exhausted to run so they were now sort of shuffling forward as best as they could manage. They fell upon the waiting canteens like a pair of starving dogs.

"Filled with sand!" Henry cursed as he poured.

Oswald did the same and then Mexicans opened fire on them from somewhere just ahead in the darkness.

Henry grunted, pitching forward with his pistol gripped in his fist. He emptied two bullets into the earth and twitched his way into eternity.

Oswald felt a bullet spin him around. He didn't even realize that he had drawn his six-gun and now was returning fire at nothing but shadows and muzzle flashes.

He lost consciousness gasping, "Natalie!"

Chapter 17

About ten miles south of Spur, Longarm had met two unsavory Americans leading burros laden with what looked like sacks of ore. Back in Spur, in addition to new clothes, he'd also managed to wangle twenty dollars in cash out of Milton Weber in his exchange for Brendon Killion's prized weapons. Now, he offered the unsavory pair of riders two dollars for information.

What he learned was worth every penny.

"We talked to a fella named Henry who was riding south. He asked if we'd seen a skinny American riding a buckskin. We told him we hadn't, but a Mexican we met on the road said he'd seen a white man on a buckskin and showed us where his tracks went south across the desert. Mister, you'd have to be blind to miss 'em."

"And what did this Henry say when you told him that?" Longarm had asked.

"Said the skinny fella he was chasin' was a damned crazy man lookin' for some girl that was probably livin' in a little farming village called Chili."

"Did the skinny fella have a name for the woman he was looking for?"

"Yep, but I forgot. Thing of it is, if the skinny fella on

that buckskin wanted a woman, he should have visited some whores. They're cheap on both sides of the border and a whole lot easier to meet."

"Where is this village called Chili?"

The men gave him directions. This news greatly lifted Longarm's low spirits because now he knew that Oswald Miller had somehow escaped the murdering women of the Black Scorpion Ranch. Not only had the Tucson lawyer survived, he must have learned that his Natalie was living in Chili.

Longarm had gladly paid the two hard cases and let them ride from his sight so they didn't back-shoot him for the rest of his money. Once he was out of their rifle range, he had sent his horse running south.

Hours later, it had been easy to see where two horses had abandoned the road and cut south into the terrible desert wasteland. Why they had left the poor road, Longarm could not imagine, but the evidence led him in the same direction.

Two days later he followed a cloud of vultures expecting to find Oswald dead. But instead, he discovered where Oswald and someone else had made their stand near a pile of rocks and cactus. The stench of death was thick as the birds of prey. The vultures were still having a feast on three unrecognizable bodies. From their clothing, Longarm could tell that two of the victims were Mexicans and the third must have been the one called Henry. Longarm made that assumption based on the fact that the American's corpse was broader in the shoulders than Oswald.

Longarm also found two canteens still half filled with sand. The explanation was obvious and so was the deadly deception. The only remaining mystery was the whereabouts of Oswald. It was plain to see that there had been many horsemen in this place and it was Longarm's opinion that they were either bandits or revolutionaries. That a tenderfoot like Oswald had somehow managed to stay alive was a real mystery.

"They're going that way," Longarm told his horse. "And by my reckoning, that would be toward Chili where Natalie might be found."

Longarm had ridden into Mexico better prepared than either Henry or Oswald. He'd brought six big canteens of water and now he removed his Stetson, poured water into it and let the animal drink. The horse was so thirsty that it gulped the pitiful amount down and then tried to lick the Stetson's wet felt in need of every last drop.

He glanced up at the sun and then back at the flock of ravaging buzzards. He should have tried to bury the human remains, but it was far too late for that and he couldn't spare the time or the energy. By tomorrow, the bones of the three dead men would be picked clean leaving only enough for the ants and insects.

It was very late in the day, but the desert heat remained intense. "We'll be in the village by midnight," he told the horse and to keep his own spirits up. "Then you'll get all the water you want and a good feed of oats. Just don't go lame on me out here."

Longarm was very worried about Oswald as he remounted and rode away. He had not covered the distance of a weak rock throw when the screeching horde of vultures returned to finish their work on the three corpses. Longarm tried to shut out the hideous sound of their fighting over human carrion as he pushed his horse into a fast trot aiming it toward the mountains he needed to cross and the village he had to find.

When Longarm rode into Chili late that night, he saw that the village was almost completely dark except for a cantina at the southern end of the dirt street. He could hear guitar music and raucous laughter. There seemed to be a lot of activity and Longarm wondered if he was riding into far more trouble than he could handle.

He found a livery with a big corral containing burros, donkeys, cattle, goats and horses. Longarm dismounted and knocked on the door of a shack. He was soon rewarded by a little old man who yawned and nodded his head in greeting. It wasn't hard to communicate to the liveryman what was needed and his horse was soon being unsaddled and given water.

"Feed him well, senor," Longarm ordered in a stern voice.

The Mexican stable owner nodded vigorously. It gave Longarm a good deal of satisfaction to see his thirsty animal drink its fill.

"Gringo?" Longarm asked.

"*Si! You* gringo!"

"No. *Another* gringo. Senor Oswald."

The man was busy with his horse and it was clear that he would rather do his duty than try to understand what Longarm was asking. He just kept shrugging his shoulders and saying, "*No comprendo*, senor. *No comprendo*."

Longarm drank from one of his canteens and then collected his rifle and saddlebags before heading toward the cantina. As he neared the cantina, he saw that there was some kind of a celebration taking place. But it didn't seem like a religious celebration and he saw only a few women among the rough-looking men.

These may be the ones that killed Henry and did something with Oswald, he thought. *I had better stay out of sight and wait to see what is really going on.*

He found a good vantage point and watched as the Mexicans drank, sang and danced. The few women among them looked terrified and there were several village men lying in the dirt, but Longarm could not tell if they were alive . . . or dead.

The tall, self-important one that appeared to be the

leader was as drunk as his men. He wore a bandoleer around his shoulder and two pistols at his side. Occasionally, he would cry out something in English although no one seemed to comprehend.

What is going on? Are they revolutionaries under General Escobar? Or simply a pack of banditos?

Longarm watched the party until his eyes grew heavy and then, against his will, he fell into an exhausted sleep.

A cock was crowing proudly when Longarm awoke to see a thin, spotted dog studying him with his head cocked sideways. When it saw that Longarm was awake, the dog wagged its tail, looking hopeful that it might be fed a scrap or at least be given a scratch behind its tattered ears.

Longarm petted the dog and it leaned in for more attention. Daylight was just starting to turn the cornfields golden and he could now plainly see that this was a poor but surprisingly large village. A shirtless man stepped out of an adobe hut nearby and walked a few feet to urinate in the street. The farmer took his time and scratched his privates earnestly. Then, he gazed at the cantina and spat in the dirt leaving no doubt that he held it in deep contempt.

Longarm would have liked to have presented himself to the villager and satisfied his intense curiosity about what was taking place in Chili but the man disappeared into his hut.

There were still bodies lying in the dirt in front of the cantina and Longarm had no idea if they were alive or dead. What he did know was that something was very much amiss. Despite the early hour and the beauty of the sunrise, Longarm could feel in his bones that there was evil and death in Chili.

He knew that the village would soon be coming awake. That women would begin the day preparing the morning meal and that men would be heading out to work in the fields. That time was fast approaching and Longarm knew that his opportunity to reach the cantina without being seen was fleeting.

I'd better get over there right now while the getting is good.

He patted the mongrel saying, "Wish me luck."

Longarm came to his feet and walked swiftly across the dirt street to the cantina. He paused only long enough to discover that most of the bodies were passed out, but that two villagers had been beaten unconscious.

He entered the cantina which was little more than a crumbling adobe hut with a thatched roof and, at the far end, a bar consisting of cracked wooden planks. Now there were men all around him on the floor and sprawled across a few tables. One of them was the leader and he was snoring as loudly as anyone.

Longarm was undecided what to do next but indecision was the last thing he needed so, when he spied a second room leading off from the one he was in, he tiptoed toward it drawing his gun.

The room was dark and dusty. It took him a minute to see through the gloom and when his eyes adjusted, he took a deep breath.

"Oswald?"

His friend had been shot. Longarm could see a dirty bandage had been pressed to his shoulder. He also had been bound to a post, hands tied behind his back. The American's head was slumped on his chest and he was either unconscious or asleep.

On a pallet on the dirt floor was another man, a Mexican, who had also been shot and wounded. This man's breathing was very ragged and shallow. Longarm would not have sworn to it but the man sounded as if a bullet had punctured one of his lungs. His future did not look very promising.

Longarm didn't have a pocketknife but almost all of

the Mexicans in the larger room carried knives of every size and description. Longarm took one from the nearest revolutionary and used it to cut his friend free. Oswald started into wakefulness and when he recognized Longarm, he opened his mouth to cry out a joyful greeting but Longarm clamped his hand over it silencing him and probably saving both their lives.

"Listen to me," he whispered. "Don't say anything. Just nod your head. Can you walk?"

A nod.

"Are you strong enough to use a gun?"

Again, a nod.

"Good," Longarm whispered, as he helped Oswald to his feet. For a moment, the lawyer leaned against him and then he seemed to find some strength.

"We've got to get you out of here fast. Let's go."

But Oswald's hand bit into Longarm's side and he hissed, "I'm not leaving Chili until I find Natalie."

Longarm could hardly believe his ears. "Look. We either get out of here fast or we die. So let's go!"

Oswald clenched his jaw and nodded with understanding. Longarm had to put his arm around the lawyer to keep him upright. Then, together, they hurried out a back door and made their way to the livery where Oswald collapsed in a pile of straw.

"I don't know if anyone saw us or not," Longarm said. "I expect a few of the villagers did. But they're probably more afraid of the revolutionaries than they are of two gringos."

"General Escobar is here," Oswald said. "He let me know that I was going to go before a firing squad this morning. When he discovers that I'm missing, they'll turn this village upside down trying to find us. We can't escape and we can't hide. Marshal, our goose is cooked."

"Don't say that," Longarm commanded. "There is a

171

corral full of horses not fifty feet away. You can still ride, can't you?"

"Back to Spur with the general and his men on our tail?"

"Yeah, if that's what it takes!" Longarm said angrily.

"Not until I find Natalie."

Longarm ran his hand wearily across his eyes. "Look," he said, giving his very best effort at being patient. "Maybe you are in so much pain or have lost so much blood that you can't think straight. But let me say this one more time . . . we have to get out of this village before those revolutionaries wake up and find you missing. We may already be out of time."

"I won't leave without at least seeing Natalie."

Longarm came to his feet. "Oswald, I'm not going to throw my own life away because you're an idiot."

"Then leave me."

"To a firing squad? What good is that to you or your precious Natalie? Alive, we can at least make a run for the border and put up a fight."

"Go then. Go now!" Oswald pleaded.

"All right, I will."

Longarm started to leave but when he reached the corral, he knew that he just couldn't leave Oswald to a firing squad. That being the case, maybe he could knock the fool unconscious and throw him over the back of a horse.

"Senor, don't move or you are a dead man!" came a voice from behind him.

Longarm would have made a dive for cover but he heard not one, but three hammers being cocked, so it seemed smart to do as he'd just been ordered.

"Gringo, put your hands high over your head."

Longarm had no choice but to obey. His gun was snatched from his holster and his rifle was tossed into the straw pile.

"Turn around slow."

Longarm did as he was told and saw three Mexicans, including the man that he had judged their leader.

"Who are you?"

Longarm had no intention of telling them that he was a United States Marshal. If he had, they'd probably have tortured him rather than have him face a quick death by a firing squad.

"I am a friend of Mr. Brendon Killion."

The leader stepped up and backhanded Longarm hard enough to almost knock him down. "Lying gringo! One more time. What are you doing here and what is your name?"

"My name is . . . is Abraham."

"Last name!"

"Lincoln."

Even in the dim light, Longarm could see the revolutionary leader's face darken with rage as he realized the pathetic joke. The man drew back his fist but Longarm struck first. Custis threw a hard right cross that broke the man's nose like dry twig and knocked him out cold. The other two Mexicans fired but Longarm was already diving for their knees. He knocked them down and in a fury he beat them senseless with their own weapons.

"Oswald," he said, "we're getting out of here right now."

The lawyer didn't argue. He stumbled after Longarm toward the corral but it was all for nothing. Shouts filled the air and suddenly, a dozen men had Longarm and Oswald surrounded.

"What now, Marshal?"

"I don't have a clue," Longarm replied as he and his friend crouched in the barn. "But I do know one thing."

"What's that?"

"Damned if I'm going to surrender so that we can be executed this morning by a firing squad."

"I need a gun," Oswald said.

Longarm gave the lawyer a pistol that he'd collected from one of the fallen Mexicans. "It probably doesn't shoot straight."

"It'll do," Oswald growled. "One thing for certain is that we're going to take some of them with us before we go down."

"That's the attitude!" Longarm shouted, ducking as bullets began to rip the livery barn apart.

Chapter 18

The gun battle at Chili continued for nearly an hour and, by then, the livery was riddled with bullet holes and both Longarm and Oswald were running dangerously low on ammunition.

"There must be some way we can get out of this alive," Longarm said, his expression grim. "But we'd better figure it out soon."

Oswald unleashed a shot. "They've got us outgunned and surrounded. It doesn't look good."

"How is your bullet wound?"

"It's not going to kill me."

Longarm studied the corral. "I'm going to have to make a try for some horses," he decided. "It's our only hope of escape."

Oswald looked doubtful. "Those guys aren't marksmen but, even so, you'd be Swiss cheese before you made it halfway to the corral."

Longarm figured Oswald was correct. "You got any better ideas? We're not going to sprout wings and fly out of this village."

"Marshal Long, I'm fresh out of ideas."

"That's what I figured."

"Did you kill those three behind us?" Oswald asked, glancing over his shoulder.

"No," Longarm replied, "but why don't you go see if they're waking up? The last thing we need is for one of them to rouse himself and stab us in the back."

"Yeah. And maybe they're carrying some ammunition."

Oswald hurried back to the three Mexicans that Longarm had managed to beat unconscious. "Holy cow!" he cried.

Longarm muttered as he crawled back to join the lawyer. "What's wrong now?"

"The first one you slugged is Vitorio Escobar."

"So?"

"He's General Escobar's brother!"

"So? He was their leader and he speaks good English but what . . ."

"Don't you get it?" Oswald cried with excitement. "We can exchange Vitorio for our lives. Those men out there will know they'll be executed if they didn't try to save the General's brother."

"Maybe General Escobar *hates* his brother."

"Yeah," Oswald admitted, his excitement fading. "Hadn't thought about that possibility. But it's worth a try, isn't it?"

Longarm ducked as three bullets splintered more wood close to his head. "Drag Vitorio out here and let's see what happens. Make sure that the other two don't wake up and catch us by surprise."

"I won't shoot them while they're knocked out cold, if that's what you mean."

"Than use the butt of your pistol to crack their heads and keep them way out in dreamland," Longarm said, returning fire and having the satisfaction of seeing a revolutionary being knocked over backward.

Moments later, Oswald dragged Vitorio forward. The

Mexican was heavy and the lawyer's wound had reopened under the dirty bandage with fresh blood.

"I should have gotten him," Longarm said, angry with himself.

"I'll be alright," Oswald replied with a grimace. "The bullet I took a few days ago just tore up the flesh and probably looks worse than it is. Vitorio is waking up."

Longarm slapped the man hard across the face three times until Vitorio's eyes popped open. He was dazed but immediately began to struggle and curse quite eloquently in both English and Spanish.

Longarm pressed the barrel of his gun to Vitorio's forehead. "Vitorio, I'm going to pull the trigger unless you shut up and do exactly what I tell you."

"What do you want, gringo?"

"We want to live and you're our ticket out of this village."

"Never!"

Longarm thumbed back the hammer of his Colt. "We have nothing to lose by killing you. Say your prayers because I'm about to send you to hell."

"Please, wait! I don't want to die, senor!"

The light was plenty strong enough now to see that Vitorio had fully regained his senses and, in fact, was sweating in terror. "I will do what you say, senor."

"That's better," Longarm answered. "All we want is for you to tell your men to stop shooting and to let us go."

"*Si!* We will let you ride back to the border."

"Sure you will," Longarm said cryptically. "Because you're going with us as our protection."

Vitorio started to object, but then he looked into Longarm's steely eyes and wisely changed his mind.

"Go ahead. Order them to stop firing and tell them that we require three saddled horses. Tell them that I will keep a gun trained on you at all times. If one of your men even looks like he wants to shoot us, you'll be the first one to die."

"I believe you," Vitorio said, licking his lips and swallowing hard. He was a large man in his late thirties, heavy in the chest with a full beard and moustache. He had probably once been slender, dashing and handsome but no more because of too much drink and food. Now, Vitorio Escobar just looked very helpless and afraid.

"One more thing," Longarm added. "Between my friend and I, we know enough Spanish to be able to tell what you say. Any tricks and you are dead."

Vitorio nodded and sat up as more bullets passed just overhead. When he shouted, his voice cracked and it carried a pleading sound rather than the ring of command. But the gunfire from around them fell silent.

"Horses. We want three saddled horses. The best in that corral."

"And canteens," Oswald added. "Along with rifles and ammunition. All tied to the saddles."

Longarm nodded, pleased that Oswald was thinking straight again and wasn't insisting on seeing Natalie. It was Longarm's considered opinion that, when a man faced almost certain death, it usually forced him to deal in cold realities.

It took the revolutionaries a half hour to comply to Vitorio Escobar's request but it seemed like an eternity. When they led three of the best horses forward, Longarm nodded with satisfaction.

"Vitorio?"

"Yes?"

"There's one more thing we require and that is for your men to stampede the other horses out of that corral so they can't follow. Tell them that if they do try to follow us back to Spur, we'll kill you. Remind them that if we kill you, General Escobar will execute all of *them*."

"They already know that," Vitorio said with unconcealed bitterness. "Otherwise, we would all be dead."

"Life is cheap in this neck of the woods," Longarm solemnly agreed. "Go ahead and give the order to stampede the horses out of that corral."

Vitorio did as he was told and when the last horse was galloping up the poor main street of Chili, Longarm figured that it was time to follow them. "Let's go. Vitorio, you're in front of Oswald. Any move to break free and . . ."

"I know. I'm a dead man."

"You learn fast," Oswald said as they emerged into the street with their guns trained on General Escobar's sweating brother.

At the same time, the villagers emerged silently from their houses. They stared as the tense standoff unfolded, women holding small children close to their skirts, men clutching their farming tools. It was clear to Longarm that the people of Chili were frightened but too curious to stay inside once the gunfire stopped. He wondered if they had seen anything in their lives to match this deadly game.

"Mount up and let's ride," Longarm ordered, knowing that if just one of the armed revolutionaries that surrounded them became foolish, they were all dead.

"Vitorio, you ride that horse," Longarm ordered, wanting him to take what looked like the poorest of the three mounts.

"That is my horse!" Vitorio spat, pointing to a tall black.

"Not anymore," Longarm said "Oswald. You ride the black and I'll take the sorrel. Let's move slow but don't stop for any reason. I'll cover you both as we leave."

"All right," Oswald said, eyes racing back and forth across the faces of the villagers.

Vitorio squared his shoulders and tried to look brave in front of what remained of his patrol, but he was badly shaken.

"Nice and easy," Longarm said. "No one has to die this morning."

They started off and were almost past the grim-faced revolutionaries when Oswald suddenly cried, "Natalie!"

"Damn," Longarm groaned as the young man leapt from the black horse and ran toward a woman who had stepped forward at the sound of her name.

Longarm didn't know what to do and even Vitorio looked confused and upset.

"It's his old childhood sweetheart," Longarm explained as the pair embraced. "Long, complicated love story."

"So that is the young woman he was willing to die for."

"Yep."

"Stupid gringo."

"I agree," Longarm said as the revolutionaries shifted nervously and everyone in the village stared at the couple.

Longarm was too far away to hear their words which were few but obviously heartfelt. He did hear Natalie sob and, when that happened, a farmer bowed his head and the two small children at his side rushed to their mother.

Natalie bent down and picked the smaller one up who was no more than a toddler. Oswald grinned and stroked the child's black hair. Then Natalie introduced the older boy.

Oswald reached into his pocket and removed a coin. He knelt by the boy's side and kissed him on both cheeks before rising. He looked at Natalie's husband, a proud but poor Mexican farmer and nodded with what Longarm guessed was approval.

A moment later, Oswald was back in the saddle. "I found her," he said raggedly to Longarm. "That was Miss Natalie Quinn."

"So I gathered. Married with two children."

"And a good husband. She told me his name was Pablo. Pablo Sanchez. And she is now Mrs. Natalie Sanchez. Her life is good but hard."

"You can tell me what you said to her when we get out of this mess," Longarm told the lawyer.

"I can tell you now," Oswald insisted. "Natalie said that she loves her family and this simple but honest village. That she has no regrets and wished me the happiness that she now has in her heart."

"That's it?"

"That's all I needed to hear," Oswald said, trying to keep his composure as they rode out of Chili with their guns trained on Vitorio.

They were not followed and when they finally reached the border, Vitorio snarled, "Now set me free."

But Longarm shook his head. "There were badly beaten villagers back there in Chili and you are responsible."

"I did not touch them!" Vitorio cried with indignation.

"Maybe not, but you are still responsible and for that, you will go to prison."

"I am a Mexican! You cannot take me out of my country and throw me in an American prison. I am the brother of General Hernandez Escobar!"

"That's right," Longarm said as they crossed the border. "And I'm a United States Marshal who has placed you under arrest."

"Vitorio is also responsible for Henry's death," Oswald said. "We were attacked, betrayed and ambushed."

Longarm didn't want to think about Henry and the vultures, so he just nodded in agreement. "I think our friend here is going to spend a long, long time in prison."

"You cannot do this! I will protest to your government. The general will protest!"

Longarm scoffed. "Your brother is nothing but a two-bit revolutionary whose grandiose plans have disappeared like smoke. Do you really think that either the legitimate government in Mexico City or our government in Washington, D.C., will care what General Escobar says or what becomes of either him or you?"

Vitorio's bravado snapped and he wept in his hands. It was a pitiful sight, but Longarm didn't care. This man was a callous bully and coward. A subjugator of helpless corn farmers and their families. And while Longarm wasn't at all sure that his own government would imprison Vitorio Escobar for very long, at least it would be some well-deserved punishment.

Their horses were played out by the time they reached the vast and powerful Black Scorpion Ranch. Zona Killion was there to greet them and she was dressed for mourning in black, which made her look all the more beautiful. Nothing was said to Longarm about his being the cause of her mother's and sister's death and that was not unexpected.

"You have been wounded again," Zona told Oswald. "You are not fit to go on to Tucson. You need my attention!"

Oswald surprised Longarm by nodding in agreement. "I would like to stay here with you."

Longarm didn't smile but Oswald's words gave him a good feeling. He had a hunch that the lawyer from Tucson was going to stay a long, long time at this ranch and that something that had been very wrong in his mind was now turning out right.

Miss Zona Killion would heal more than Oswald's physical wounds. She would finally heal his broken heart.

Watch for

Longarm and the Bad Girls of Rio Blanco

296th novel in the exciting LONGARM series
from Jove

Coming in July

Explore the exciting Old West with one of the men who made it wild!

WILDGUN

THE HARD-DRIVING WESTERN SERIES
FROM THE CREATORS OF *LONGARM*

Jack Hanson

Round 'em all up!